AMERICAN BLOOD

AMERICAN BLOOD

BY

BRUCE WOODS

www.penmorepress.com

American Blood by Bruce Woods
Copyright © 2020 Bruce Woods

ISBN-13: 978-1-950586-65-3(Paperback)
ISBN :-978-1-950586-64-6(e-book)

BISAC Subject Headings:
FIC031020FICTION / Thrillers / Historical
FIC009100 FICTION / Fantasy / Action & Adventure
FIC009070 FICTION / Fantasy / Dark Fantasy

Edited by Chris Paige
Cover Illustration by
The Book Cover Whisperer:
ProfessionalBookCoverDesign.com
Address all correspondence to:

Penmore Press LLC
920 N Javelina Pl
Tucson AZ 85748

DEDICATION

For Mary, Ethan, and Alice, yet again.

Disclaimer

This is a work of the imagination and the characters created for it are, you know, fictional, and not meant to represent anyone living, dead, or undead. If any of them remind you of yourself or someone you know, you have my congratulations—or sympathy—depending upon the character involved. It is also a work of historical fiction, however, and much research has gone into accurately representing the times and places portrayed. That said, when an historical person in this work interacts with a fictional one, the result is wholly a figment of my imagination. I do not mean to imply how that real individual did, or would, react to vampires, spirits, or other such entities.

As also noted, I've gone to some lengths to research the period in which this novel is set, and hope that for the most part it will pass historical muster. The few remaining Steampunk elements, although sometimes quite nifty, are also pure fancy. Dutiful historians will note that in some instances the chronology of the book will intentionally depart from historical accuracy to serve the needs of the story. Any unintentional errors are the fault of the author and not of the various editors who have done so much to give this story whatever charm it might have.

Finally, fiction or no, this work owes a great debt to our frighteningly recent historical past. If any readers are moved to go on and learn more about such incredible women as Alice Paul, Victoria Woodhull, and the others who suffered so much for suffrage, I'll consider that obligation at least in part paid.

Bruce Woods

Monsters exist, but they are too few in number to be truly dangerous. More dangerous are the common men, the functionaries ready to believe and to act without asking questions.
—Primo Levi

Dr. Gannon told me I must be fed. ...I was held down by five people... Gannon pushed the tube up left nostril... It hurts nose and throat very much and makes nose bleed freely... Operation leaves one very sick.
—Lucy Burns

CHAPTER 1

These brick walls are either cold or hot. In the winter, the chill aches its way through them. They hold onto it like misers, and no form of heating can warm them. In the summer, they enclose ovens, and the air within grows still and stifling and thick with stink. Spring and fall are gone before their transitions can be felt.

The aims of the institution's planners were lofty. They set out to create a facility that would reduce recidivism among the purveyors of minor and often victimless crimes. The plan was to let these men and women work for a living, often in the healthful outdoors, by building and provisioning the very prison that held them. This system would, the dreamers imagined, improve the health of people used to living on the edge of society, and instill in them a positive ethic at the same time.

It might have been better if the planners had given a little additional thought to the thermal properties of the bricks with which the prisoners surrounded themselves. Bureaucrats to a man, and limited in imagination, the designers would certainly not have ever suspected that the very facility of which they had dreamed, labyrinthine and intricately managed, was like a dinner bell to a certain manner of creature who bores into such a system early, establishes a fiefdom within it, and draws strength from it like a leech.

When this story opens, he had already been there for some time, and established himself as the prison's lord and master. It had been easy. As if he had been made for maneuvering and manipulating the endlessly relabeled doors and drawers of bureaucracy. Now, with his goal achieved, he could relax and enjoy the spoils.

Even before the facility began to go downhill, when the crops that the inmates raised were not yet sold at the open market, and the prisoners were fed the worst that could be bought; when the rats had not yet begun to fight for the right of a place in the bedrooms, there had been pain. Any of incarceration is an incubator of hurt, whether from the fear for the daughter left alone outside, or the sprain or bruise from an altercation with a guard or another prisoner. And agony is what he fed upon.

He was quick to learn, that by reducing the quality of life within the institution, he could increase profitability while enhancing the suffering which he so enjoyed. For years he did so, a worm in the heart of the great Workhouse, quietly drinking in the pain surrounding him and slowly growing in power.

Sometimes he allowed himself to enjoy the gamier flavors of more direct participation. There were always those deserving punishment, and when it was necessary to make a strong statement he would inflict such correction himself. There was salt for his meal in these acts, a savor less noticeable in the more passive feedings and it brought some variety to his days.

It was a pleasant existence; everything that he needed was his. Yet his diet, though healthful, was predictable and bland. He had thrived on what amounted to rice and beans for years; then by chance, the world outside his walls twisted and he tasted steak. It may well have been that simple event that brought the two of us together.

I discovered much of this after the fact, and continue to explore the issue. It seems that, however often time attempts to teach me otherwise, I cannot resist putting my fingers into dark places. Thankfully, I've only thus far learned where he was, not where he *is*.

In fact, the sole reason for knowing his whereabouts at any given moment is to try to be elsewhere. Going forward, a portion of my art and artifice will always be reserved for maintaining a position either beyond or beneath his notice. I understand that chance is a fickle mistress, and only a fool counts upon enjoying her favors a second time.

CHAPTER 2

I knew nothing about these events as they were first unfolding, as I was to be drawn toward them by another avenue entirely.

It was an unlikely road indeed. At that stage in my existence I was far more familiar with suffering than suffrage, having been both the cause and the recipient of much of the former. My recent experiences on the world stage had also reduced any empathy I might have had for mortal concerns. Though I had taken human lovers of both sexes and was fully capable of discerning the beauty and goodness of individuals, the race of men had revealed itself to me time and again as cruel, false, and driven by blind self-interest.

Furthermore, my Kin (or "vampires" in the lexicon of the penny dreadfuls, a medium in which I confess I indulge with an enthusiast's perversity) have little interest in the campaign for women's rights. Or in voting, for that matter Rather, age and wisdom are the qualities that distribute authority among us. There are, of course, still disagreements among equals, but these are typically resolved with Socratic debate or rarely by individual combat rather than anything so crude and indiscriminate as majority rule.

Indeed, since my return to my home in Washington D.C., my chief concerns had been with establishing my position in the American community of Kin, and overseeing the considerable wealth my adventures had brought me. Under the right circumstances, money will reproduce itself more rapidly than even the mosquitoes that haunt the reclaimed swampland of my chosen city. I had learned well under the guidance of Cecil Rhodes who, though mortal, had few equals in the business of inspiring wealth to beget wealth...

As I went about this business, the question of women's suffrage seemed to be on every lip. In those early days of the twentieth century, though Iceland had long since instituted universal voting and women had earned that privilege in a handful of American states, the bulk of the nation still seemed determined to relegate its distaff citizens to the kitchen and the bedroom. An increasingly vocal cadre of women, however, was equally bent upon opening ballot boxes across America to those of their gender.

Such concerns could not have seemed more distant from my own. The task of managing my fortune filled much of my time, and what was left was typically consumed in satisfying my hunger and the other pedestrian physical desires that my transformation seems to have in no way weakened. This proved a far easier task as the ability of my eyes to Entrance continued to evolve.

It is that all-too-human libido that must own the blame for my subsequent involvement in mortal politics. It was certainly not the first—nor, I'm sure, the last—time that a great advancement in human rights was precipitated by a tug on the leash of lust.

Before I tell that tale, however, it might be appropriate to provide some information concerning my reintegration into the world of the American Kindred following my return from England more than a decade ago. Lady Ellen Terry, "immortal" stage beauty and leader of London's Kin, had provided the impetus for my earlier African and Asian adventures and had bestowed the wealth that I'd accrued as a result. More valuable than the riches, however, was the support she provided me upon my return to my native land.

Those unfamiliar with my background will probably benefit from knowing that my initiation into the ranks of the so-called undead was accidental (how it still irks me to write those words), and thus in violation of the strict rules that prevent any increases in population that might threaten our anonymity. Thus, there was no little risk associated with my revealing myself to my American compatriots.

However, so spirited was Lady Terry's championing of my cause, and so highly was she regarded despite being from a nation that many Americans, and not a few of this nation's Kin, still viewed with suspicion, that I was not only allowed to continue to exist but, was also given my home city as my own fiefdom. Despite being the nation's capital, Washington had previously been thought not cosmopolitan enough to deserve its own live-in Mistress. I established myself in a residential hotel with only my fortune and the great bronze cross of the winding key from my dear, lost Horace Wilkershire Coilcycle, displayed on my mantel like a candelabra, to remind me of my recent past.

The actual story of my making is a tale for another time and place. Suffice to say that the two responsible—one for draining me to the point of death and the other for the blood that accidentally remade me—received punishments in keeping with their roles, but tempered by the fact that there had been no intent to circumvent the rules of the Tribe. I had made no attempt to contact either of them (I had no wish to relive an event that I cannot recall to this day without anger), and they had apparently been quite happy thus far to have had no further truck with yours truly. This was soon to change.

I did reach out to other members of the community of Kin, forming friendships that have lasted to this day. Chief among these was my relationship with Mamie Clover, Mistress of the Midwest, and my champion in early days. She has since become something of a peer. With my position in society clarified, I was able to focus upon furnishing my lodgings in a manner appropriate to my position, and then to shepherding my investments to assure a long and comfortable future.

The world was not, of course, perfect. The beauties and wonders of the steam age were already disappearing in the face of the bullying ascent of the internal combustion engine, as the bemused genius of the former fell before the ruthless entrepreneurship of the latter. I mourned this, as I have a weakness for all things lovely, but that regret did not prevent me from profiting from the very changes I rued.

It was all quite pleasant, really, and would likely have continued to be without drama for some time had I not diverted my course one evening to investigate a disturbance. A young woman was speaking in an impassioned manner and she had attracted a small crowd, mostly male, many of whom seemed to take virulent issue with her contentions. As I grew nearer, I caught the sharp scent of impending violence that is obvious to the nose of any predator, and thought I noticed a vague shimmering in the air. I am no person's heroine, and was still only curious, but I did quicken my pace.

CHAPTER 3

The woman in question was tall and robust; not at all portly, but voluptuous in the feminine manner counted most appealing at that time. She was quite animated in gesture and was clad all in white, her dress rather shapeless—after the fashion of the day (but interrupting its drape nicely upon contact with the active curves within)—with a luxuriant mane of scandalously red hair spilling over her shoulders. Her eyes were May-sky blue, and her pale redhead's complexion was saved from any hint of undead morbidity by a pair of irrepressible dimples. I judged her to be close in age to myself at the time of my turning, and attractive enough, to cause me to linger.

It was immediately evident from the sign she carried (which read, "Mr. President, how long must women wait for liberty?") that the speaker was a suffragist, and that the topic of her presentation had inflamed the ire of a number of those in her audience.

She spoke with animation and clear conviction, but little drama or emotion. I had the sense that she believed that her point of view was the only possible correct one, and that she was impatient for her audience to acknowledge the fact. I daresay a more theatrical approach might have better won over this crowd. She had a striking and sensual beauty that would have ensnared a male audience, had verbal seduction been her aim. Instead, she seemed determined to win them over by force of logic alone, which I'd learned was sometimes a reach too far when dealing with mortals of either gender.

And so it seemed about to prove. As she carried heroically on, raising her voice as necessary to be heard above the heckling, it was only a matter of who would stoop to throwing the first stone. Indeed, as I reached the fringes of the crowd, I spied a young jackanapes bending over to retrieve a scrap of cobble, no doubt hoping to inspire general mayhem. The air around him seemed briefly displaced, as a photographic slide will blur when slipped out of focus.

I don't know why I acted at all. The woman was certainly attractive, but perhaps a bit fleshy for my tastes and I was not feeling particularly amorous. Regardless, as the lad stooped to pick up his stone, I contrived to knock him into the gentleman immediately in front of him. Fortune was with me, for as the boy scrabbled to maintain his balance, his right hand landed upon the gent's rear pocket, in which that worthy carried his wallet.

With a cry of anger, the accosted squire turned and seized the boy, shouting for the police. The crowd turned its attention and anger toward this more interesting altercation, no doubt motivated by the fact that pick-pocketing was recognized as a ubiquitous scourge in the Capital. While they were so occupied, I offered the suffragist an elbow which the Force of my eyes (I had slipped my tinted glassed down on my nose as I approached her, though I did not then think to turn my unfiltered gaze to our surroundings) forbade her to refuse, and led her away, chatting about nonsense as we went with an air of calm gentility.

We had only taken a few steps before she threw off the Enchantment, which had been no stronger than it needed to be, and withdrew her arm from mine in confusion.

"I'm sorry," she said, clearly flustered, "do I know you?"

"You do not," I said. "My name is Paulette Monot. And there is no need to thank me. I simply couldn't bear the thought of your getting blood on that dress. It would never have come out."

She sniffed.

"Lucy Burns," she said, "and I can assure you I've handled worse without need of rescue. Are you with NAWSA, then?"

I must have looked puzzled (the popular preoccupation with acronyms still seemed gauche to me at the time, and I had not kept myself current), for she continued before I could reply.

"The National American Woman Suffrage Association," she said. "But your confusion gives you away, and I can see that you are not. We're always in need of volunteers." Here she surveyed my attire, which was in keeping with my wealth and station. "Or donors," she added.

Though her cause did not interest me, I found myself intrigued by Miss Burns' dedication and bravery, as well as by her beauty. She seemed unaffected by her recent exposure to what had seemed clear danger of physical harm, and chattered eagerly on about her organization and the need to promote Suffrage through demands for national recognition of women's voting rights, rather than the frustratingly slow state-by-state efforts heretofore championed. Since my financial situation was comfortable and likely to improve, I allowed that I could certainly manage a regular contribution. She grew still more animated.

"You must accompany me to our office," she said. "We can formalize the details of your donation there, and I'll introduce you to my friend, Alice Paul, who spearheads our efforts." The redhead's smile would have appeared sly were it not disarmed by her dimples. "Perhaps after meeting her, you'll be persuaded to aid us with your energy as well as with your charity."

I doubted this, but seeing that I was already in for a penny, I decided to go in for a pound and agreed to accompany the suffragist to her destination. The term "office" was, I soon discovered, a rather grandiose appellation for the place to which Miss Burns led me. This "headquarters," which apparently served as a dwelling place for Miss Burns and Miss Paul as well as their center of operations, was actually a shopworn basement apartment commendable only for its proximity to the White House.

Alice Paul was far more noteworthy. In stature and appearance she was quite the opposite of her companion. She was petite and slender where the other was tall and voluptuous, and gifted with large and soulful violet eyes where Miss Burns' were of a more common blue. Rather than the latter's flaming red locks, her hair was dark and thick, and seemed in eminent danger of breaking free from the prison of the hat perched atop it.

She was speaking on the telephone as we entered. I was stricken by the ease with which this young woman employed a device that I still regarded with the caution one might employ when handling a venomous snake. It was a reminder that, though we might look to be of an age, I had retained that appearance for almost two decades. Moreover, I would continue to do so while she was only stopping there briefly on her journey toward death. It is strange to remember that such revelations had so recently the power to surprise me!

She spoke rapidly, her words distinct and without noticeable accent or inflection. There was no indication that she felt that the machine hindered her communication in any way. I had the sense that she used her voice not as an actress would, to convey emotion and solicit empathy, but rather as a typewriter or some other machine designed to capture and disseminate information clearly and with efficiency. Perhaps she had indoctrinated Lucy Burns in this manner, as the brusqueness seemed for more natural to the brunette than it did to her more extravagant companion.

With the call finished, the little woman returned the earpiece to its hook and, finger already poised to dial anew, glanced up to see Miss Burns and me standing before her. Her attention focused solely upon the former.

"You're back rather soon," she said. "Am I to assume that you ran into difficulty?"

The redhead laughed bitterly. It was a tight little chortle, clearly flavored by broad experience with the contrariness of men.

"I chanced upon an audience that was less than receptive to my message," she said. "They might even have stooped to violence, had not Miss Monot here swooped to my rescue, though I'm unclear as to exactly how she did. More important though, she is willing to make a donation to our cause."

Now the great violet eyes alighted upon me, and I watched as the woman's delicate features tightened with what might have been distaste. Although I had never before encountered such perception in a mortal woman or man, I knew immediately that she saw me for what I was.

"That is most generous of Miss Monot," she said, still addressing the redhead. "Perhaps you'll allow us a little time in private. I wish to thank her properly for her assistance and perhaps delve into other ways in which she might aid our efforts?"

With a smile that spoke of her faith in her friend's powers of persuasion, Miss Burns excused herself and stepped into the adjoining kitchen, announcing her intention to refresh herself with a cup of tea. As she left, she pulled the door closed behind her, and Alice Paul and I were alone.

"You should know that I am not frightened by you," she began as soon as our privacy was assured. And indeed she did not seem to be, though I had no doubt that she would be helpless were I to attempt to do her harm.

"You have no need to be," I answered, not a little put out. "I keep well fed enough without imposing upon strangers, and have only followed my curiosity here. How is it, though, that you perceive my nature, an ability I had not known possible among mortals?"

"I would answer you if I could," she said, "but alas, I cannot. I have, since my youth, been aware of things invisible to my peers. I believe there have been men and woman all through history with this knowing, though they have ever been few in number. Indeed, you are not the only miraculous being that it's been my misfortune to encounter of late."

I glanced about me, half expecting to find the room crowded with creatures of mythology, but we were alone.

"More to the point," she continued, and I could clearly see the singleness of purpose that drove her, "are you indeed interested in the cause that we champion? For I was unaware that a concern for mortal politics could survive upon the far side of the grave."

I confess I found her familiarity offensive, and answered curtly.

"You were correct in that assumption. As I said, it was only curiosity that led me here, though I will honor the pledge of a donation that I made to your compatriot."

Miss Paul stood behind her desk, revealing her height to be close to mine, and thus on the smaller end of the spectrum of American women of her time.

"And yet you *were* a woman," she said. "Did not your lack of full citizenship rankle while you lived?"

"I am a woman still," I replied, somewhat huffily, "only of another sort than you. And before my making, I was more concerned with the pursuit of pleasure and things material than with politics, predilections that have followed me, as you so elegantly put it, to 'the far side of the grave.'"

I was surprised to find myself almost in debate with this woman, and apparently she felt the same, for she took a deep breath and proceeded in a more conciliatory tone.

"Any offense was unintended," she began. "You are the first of the otherworldly that I have encountered who is not clearly opposed to our efforts. Your active allegiance would be most welcome, Mrs. Monot."

"I am not wed," I continued, a little mollified, "and you may call me Paulette. We shall see what additional aid, if any, I might offer. Your cause means little to me, but perhaps you will enlighten me about the other creatures that you claim have taken an interest?"

The little brunette studied me before replying. Though I have often been counted beautiful by those of both genders, I detected not the slightest physical interest from her, despite the fact that I was dressed in a fashion calculated to call attention to my charms. I endured her gaze, posing gracefully under its attention out of habit, and awaited her reply.

After a moment, during which she perhaps considered the wisdom of revelation, she spoke again.

"I confess I do not know the proper term for them," she said, "so I call them simply 'shades.' They are not as substantial as you, although I can see them clearly. They appear in the forms of both men and women, and seem to be bent upon nothing but obstructing the ambitions of the living. There is a bitterness to their nature, which they perhaps salve by encouraging the animosity of those still upon this earthly plane. In my experience, they seem limited to influencing the mortals rather than acting upon them directly." Then she added, as if an afterthought, "And you may call me Alice, if you insist upon such informality."

Though I had no experience with the creatures she described, I did not doubt her. How could I, when I had already encountered dragons and worse? Also, I had heard tales of similar restless entities, purportedly humans who had died with too much left undone, and who rode a desire for revenge or completion into a ragged afterlife.

"How do these beings seek to confound you, Alice?" I asked, using her name deliberately so as to taste it upon my tongue, and also because I believed it would irk her.

"They make no direct assault upon me," she said. "Indeed, I think them incapable of anything other than engendering fear and hatred; I suspect even the transfer of real information is beyond them. In this way they influence our opponents, appearing to them to be the inner voices of reason or the calls of their sterner natures. I do not doubt but that some of the men who threatened Miss Burns today were acting upon the insidious suggestions of these creatures."

"Perhaps if I could see them for myself?" I said.

"We are planning a parade in advance of Wilson's inauguration," she said, sitting again and removing the telephone earpiece from its hook in preparation for another call. "Miss Burns can provide you with the details when she arranges for your donation. March with us, *Paulette*, and if your eyes can indeed perceive the shades, I believe you'll get your wish."

CHAPTER 4

Lucy—we were soon on an easy first-name basis, she being less reserved than Alice Paul—proved equal to both tasks, arranging my contribution and enthusiastically informing me about the details of the upcoming event and the part that I might play in it.

The parade was to be organized in contingents, each presenting a central theme. In those days before mass media and the other changes I've seen since, such processions were considered an art form, and the best way to convey simple concepts to a mass audience. The first group would be made up of suffragists of other nations, illustrating the fact that their battle was not solely an American struggle. The second would consist of floats and tableaus, presenting almost a moving theater and banking on the fact that drama is often more convincing than logic. The third wave, which I would occupy, was to represent women of many occupations. I learned that I would wear the sash of "Financier," and greeted that revelation with no little satisfaction.

March third, the date of the event, dawned bright and clear. Winter and spring contested for control of its temperatures, which were chill in early morning, but warmed as the day progressed. I had selected a sheath dress in the Delphos style with highlights of cochineal and indigo, the latter accentuating my blond hair and fair complexion. A straw hat with a satin band complimenting my gown provided protection from the sun.

The clinging silk of the dress displayed my form to good advantage, and if I were not the best dressed among the exotic songbirds participating in the march, I was confident that I would earn my share of appreciative glances. This was particularly so since many of the women had seen fit to hide their finery beneath coats during the chilly morning, while I was insensitive to such a small variation in temperature.

And in spite of the scourge of outerwear, what a lovely flock we made! I was later to learn that there were some eight thousand of us in the procession, a tribute to the organizational skills of the little brown-haired Napoleon who had personally supervised every detail of the event. The procession was slow in getting underway due to the number of marchers involved. It was led by Inez Milholland Boissevain, a twenty-seven-year-old attorney and famous beauty, crowned and clad all in white with a streaming cape of that same hue, who sat astride a magnificent brute of a white horse named Grey Dawn.

So costumed and mounted, Mrs. Boissevain was an inspiring presence, and lent an air of dignity to the procession that could not but be felt by the spectators. The size of that audience was beyond accounting—I've heard estimates as high as eighty thousand. People had flocked into the capital to view Wilson's inauguration, scheduled for the following morning. The bleachers that had been set up for the upcoming event were filled with paying customers a day early, profiting the concessionaire and, thanks to Alice's negotiations, the suffragists alike.

The numbers of police present were clearly inadequate to control such a crowd, and many of those authorities clung to antiquated beliefs about the proper roles of women, so I suppose it was inevitable that all would not go well.

As the parade progressed, the crowd pressed ever closer, and it became clear to me that a disturbance was in the offing. There were shouted insults, which included the usual suggestions that our time would be better spent over a stove; nor those, often slurred (for there is a class of man who considers a morning without liquor as poor as a day without sunshine), which either questioned the gender of the marchers or accused them of indulging in Sapphic love. How the latter had come to be considered an insult was ever a puzzle to me; does one limit oneself to a diet of steak when there's lobster on the table, too? None of these outbursts were unexpected, and indeed Lucy had predicted such.

I was glancing about, hoping for a glimpse of Miss Paul's shades, initially without success. I did occasionally note a shimmer in the air similar to the heat haze that will distort a distant prospect on a summer afternoon. These became more frequent as the mood of the crowd worsened. On a whim, I removed the tinted glasses from my eyes, and was suddenly able to see the creatures that I'd sought.

CHAPTER 5

This was not the first time that I'd noticed the peculiar filtering effect of these simple, blue-tinted lenses. I'd known them to limit the Entrancement my eyes were capable of, and to hide the level of my power from other Kin. It's said that Magic is merely Science that we don't yet understand. I have great respect for the geniuses of the day, but until they accept the existence of such beings as myself and those shades, there is little hope that they will be able to explain the mechanics of this curious capability in what is only, after all, colored glass.

As soon as I saw the creatures, my sense of trepidation evaporated, and I wondered if that feeling here, and previously when Lucy was in danger, was the work of these ethereal whisperers as much as of my own intuition. Regardless, it was immediately clear that they knew that I could see them. I suspected that the curious power of my glasses had prevented them from perceiving my nature as surely as it had hidden them from me. (Though the lenses had shown no such ability to hide me from Miss Paul, whose "seeing" was apparently of another sort entirely.)

At first, the creatures recoiled from my glance as if in fright, but soon enough one among their number approached me. He (for it took the form of a man) moved through the marchers around me as gracefully as fog through a forest. None of them were even slightly aware of his presence, though he certainly influenced their thoughts. At last, he and I were side by side.

As Alice Paul had reported, the shade appeared not quite as solid as any of those mortals around me, and he easily passed through spectators who stood in his way. His form was that of a burly man, extravagantly mustached, in a dark wool boiler suit and bowler hat. His demeanor was cruel and aggressive, and he towered over me as he spoke, his lips moving but the words manifesting themselves in my mind and not my ears.

'You do not belong here, blood sucker,' he "said," 'why do you choose to meddle in the affairs of the living, and act as if their concerns are in any way your own?'

I felt no fear, but that might have been a product of my own unholy self-confidence rather than a rational reaction. Never having encountered his like before, I determined to test my capabilities against him and directed a strong Enchantment at the entity to see if I could bend it to my will.

This produced no effect whatsoever. In fact, it seemed that the shade was unaware altogether of my attempt, so I decided instead to try to engage it in conversation. Since I could not speak aloud to it without being overheard by the marchers around me and causing them to question my sanity, I stared at the apparition and *thought* my reply.

'It would seem that your intent is more clearly to meddle than mine,' I said, simply forming the words in my mind, 'What do you call yourselves, and what is your purpose here?'

The creature appeared to swell with anger. He clearly enjoyed some pride of place among his companions, and I suspected he found my lack of fear both surprising and frustrating. The level of the thought-voice rose to a bellow, as if he could intimidate me by bluster alone.

'We are *Souls*,' he roared. 'We are those who rise when the flesh falls. And we do not answer to you, a thing of dead meat with no way to harm us.'

I found this characterization most unflattering, for though my flesh is chill, I certainly feel more alive in this form than I ever did as a mortal girl. Yet I also sensed that part of what he said was true: I was quite without a weapon with which to threaten this thing.

'It seems that we are at an impasse then, Soul,' I thought, 'For you are no more able to influence me than I can harm you. Though I caution you, I am stubborn and resourceful. Do not assume that your immunity will last forever.'

'It will last until our chore is done, dead woman.' The last was accompanied by a sneer of distaste. 'And that is time enough for such as us.'

With that, he drifted back into the crowd of spectators, which had by now pressed so close on every side as to bring the parade to a halt. The roar of the mob increased in volume, whipped as it undoubtedly was by the invisible horsemen who straddled its minds, and then the first stone flew.

American Blood

As the mood became more violent, my first objective was to assess any danger to myself. Some may condemn me for this instinctual self-preservation; but resilient as my Kind are, we are not invulnerable. The "immortal" who is not ever aware of the dangers surrounding her can become very mortal very soon.

In this instance, however, it was clear that there was little risk to me. Though the Souls had undoubtedly urged the mob to disrupt the parade, its violence was limited to pushing the marchers and destroying their signs. I say this not to belittle the seriousness of the outrage, for some women were certainly injured when the shoving became too enthusiastic, but to explain the lack of danger to myself.

It is always difficult, when in public and facing a hazardous situation, to determine how best to react while keeping one's nature undercover. Here, I did little, but when a policeman charged to protect the parade instead advanced upon the marchers with truncheon drawn. I caught him with my eyes and found it easy to turn his cruel attentions back upon his fellow aggressors.

The authorities were clearly part of the problem. In most cases I think it was more a matter of their numbers being inadequate to control the crowds they were faced with than any actual violence directed toward the suffragists. Eventually, a cavalry troop which the inestimable Miss Paul had arranged to have on call anticipating (and perhaps hoping for) just this sort of disaster, was able to clear the way and the parade struggled on to its terminus only somewhat the worse for wear.

The two lovely ringleaders counted it quite a success. The numbers involved were certainly impressive, and the injuries and tales of brutality (I learned that upwards of two hundred were treated for one form of wound or another, though none of these were judged to be life-threatening) insured far more media coverage than a peaceful parade, no matter how large, would have generated. I was more concerned with the mystery of the Souls and what actions they might take in the future than I was with mere publicity.

It was some time before I was able to get a moment alone with Alice. She was involved in drafting and distributing a seemingly endless string of press releases detailing the parade; the inadequacies of the police protection; and the actual assaults upon her marchers at the hands of those charged with their protection. In truth, I thought that she exaggerated the latter instances in many of these reports in order to play up the sort of outrages most likely to generate newspaper attention. There can be no doubt that this approach was successful. Even the journals unfriendly to the suffragists' cause (including the stately *New York Times*) ran pieces sympathetic to "the poor women" who had been manhandled by police and rude street toughs. The struggle for suffrage was often as much about social class as gender, and Miss Paul was happy to allow her society women to be roughed up by "the lower sort of men" if it generated interest in the cause.

Once the initial firestorm of media had abated, however, I did once again find myself alone with Miss Paul in her tiny office in the F Street basement apartment and was able to share with her what I had learned.

"Did you see them, then?" she asked me, looking up from a typewriter that appeared as weary as she. Indeed, the woman looked to be even more frail than usual, and her strange eyes were fever-bright. I thought I could see evidence of the damage to her constitution by the ill handling she'd endured on her hunger strike while supporting the Pankhursts in England. Later events, however, were to convince me that she judged such horrors as little more than additional bolts in her quiver.

"I did," I replied, "and actually spoke to one, if such communication can rightly be called speech. They call themselves 'Souls,' and believe that they are the spirits of the dead. Their goal is clearly the failure of your enterprise, though whether their animosity is directed at your cause or at you yourself I am as yet unable to determine."

"Alas," the brunette replied, "I'd feared it so, but what objection could such shades have to our enfranchisement?"

"I'm not at all certain that they are what they claim," I said. "Perhaps they are simply the manifestations of some particularly fierce malevolence, mortal or otherwise, stirred up to counter your ambitions. Tell me, Alice Paul, have you earned any enemies whose animosity seems an outsized reaction to whatever harm you might have done them?"

She considered this carefully before replying.

"Our struggle has been a long one," she began, "spanning generations. There are those in the leadership of NAWSA who believe that the route to suffrage is through individual action by the states, rather than through an overriding federal amendment. Many of these women have dedicated their careers to this struggle, and resent the appearance of younger individuals such as Miss Burns and myself, who firmly believe that the latter approach is the only one that might bring success within our lifetimes."

"Is there," I asked, "a particular person in whom this animosity is centered?"

"I hesitate to say so," Alice replied, "for I believe the goal is all and am wary of anything that would divide our forces, but Carrie Chapman Catt, NAWSA's president, seems to harbor a dislike for me all out of proportion to our differences. That said, I find it hard to believe that she would risk harm to the movement in order to counter my efforts."

At this point Lucy, who had slipped in from the kitchen through a door left ajar and had clearly overheard the tail of our conversation, chimed in.

"Carrie Catt purely hates us and you know it, Alice," she said. "She fears that we will succeed where she has failed, and steal all of the credit for obtaining suffrage, pushing her off of the stage that she so dearly enjoys."

The little brunette jumped to her feet and rounded upon her friend. If I had doubted the presence of steel in her small and slender frame, here was evidence of it aplenty.

"The door was closed, Miss Burns!" she said. "I *will* have my time alone! We cannot all be as cavalier about matters of personal privacy as you seem to be."

Though clearly taken aback, the redhead did not allow herself to be intimidated.

"It was not fully closed, Alice. And I cannot read your mind, though you sometimes seem to think you can see into mine. What I said is true, and no amount of pique on your part will make it less so. Besides, I came in to tell Paulette that she has a visitor, and he is making some of the other women uncomfortable."

The premonitions of danger I'd felt during the parade paled before the sensations produced by those words. I stepped to the door and threw it open. I saw him there, hip perched against a desk, lounging with a perfect grace that left the mortal beauties around him looking as drab as weeds struggling at the foot of a rose.

I recognized him. A lady does not soon forget the man who killed her.

CHAPTER 6

My every instinct was to prepare for combat. I felt my muscles draw and tighten, though I knew him to be older than I. I also recognized that any physical altercation between us would surely be fatal for several of the women in the room.

He showed no animosity, however. He pushed himself to his feet, the grace in that simple motion branding him as Kin, though I already knew him for what he was.

"Paulette, isn't it?" he said. "You look far better than when I last saw you."

I was very aware of Alice Paul and Lucy behind me, as well as the other women in the office, or I would perhaps have spoken more directly. As it was, I'm sure Miss Paul was chafing over this interruption to suffrage work despite the fact that she surely recognized his nature, while Lucy was likely brimming with curiosity about my mysterious (and, though it irks me no end to admit it, beautiful) caller.

"I don't recall that we were ever properly introduced," I said, making an effort to keep my voice free of inflection. "Of course I know your name. What I don't know is what business there could be between us."

"I've heard that you've become quite wealthy," he said, brushing his dark-honey hair back with one hand and clearly as comfortable as a cat in the sun. "It seems to me that I should be rewarded for the little part I played in your recent successes."

I heard a quick intake of breath behind me (I assume it was Lucy) just before I walked wordlessly past my visitor, out the apartment door and into the street. I could only hope that he would follow, for his lack of discretion would surely make further discussion in the presence of the suffragists impossible. Fortunately, trail after me he did, and so closely at my heels that he drew back in surprise when I suddenly spun to accost him.

"I owe you nothing!" I hissed. "An argument could be made that you owe your continued miserable existence to the success I managed to make of your error. You may have age on me, but I am not without friends, and I swear to you that if you wish to make a conflict of this you will encounter difficulties beyond your imagining."

He ignored my threat and favored me with a paternal smile. "I see you wish to keep your nature secret from your new mortal companions. You understand what sort of leverage this provides me? We'll speak again soon, I promise you. Until then, *au revoir*, my sweet." He walked off without looking back, a dance in miniature performed with every step.

I turned to reenter the apartment and almost ran into Lucy. She had clearly followed me out (though I did not think closely enough to have overheard our exchange) and even now watched the Kin's retreat with wide blue eyes.

"He's dangerous, isn't he?" She twirled a strand of red hair on one index finger as she spoke, and her voice was soft and unaware, as if she murmured in her sleep.

"If you want danger," I said to her, still steeped in my own anger, "go back to the park and make some more speeches. At least there's a chance that something good might come of that."

She trailed me into the apartment contritely, but only after following my adversary with her eyes until he was quite out of sight.

Alice was on the telephone when we returned, but she covered her mouthpiece with one hand and addressed me sternly.

"I trust you'll not let personal matters interfere with suffrage business again, Miss Monot." I rolled my eyes at the surname, noting that she seemed more comfortable with this formal mode of address than with the implied intimacy of given names. I also noticed that she appeared quite unruffled by Card's appearance, despite knowing him for what he was.

"I didn't invite him, Alice," I replied, purposely cleaving to the familiar. "And if I have my way, I will not see him again, here or anywhere. But to return to the matter we were discussing before his rude interruption, perhaps it would be beneficial were I to have a conversation with this Carrie Chapman Catt?"

Having overheard only the tail end of that discussion before interrupting it, Lucy glanced from the brunette to me in confusion. "Why would Paulette want to speak with Carrie Catt?" she said.

Alice Paul glanced at me, and spoke a few words into the phone before hanging up. Only then did she answer her friend. "It seems that Miss Monot believes that Mrs. Catt may have some insight into the resistance our efforts have met with of late."

Saying that, Alice took up the phone once more. I realized, as I watched with a critical eye, that she used a telephone with the grace and aggression of a fencer wielding an epée. She was able to ascertain in short order where the NAWSA president was staying and soon thereafter had the other woman on the line to arrange my visit. It was clearly a chilly conversation, though I could hear but one side of it. It was only after Miss Paul had described my recent contribution that her superior apparently warmed to the prospect of meeting me. The little brunette closed out the call with exaggerated formality, and jotted an address on a scrap of paper.

"Mrs. Catt will be in her rooms for another two hours," she said, handing me the note. "She would welcome the opportunity to meet with such a generous proponent of our cause."

"I promise to comport myself in a ladylike manner," I said, and, nodding my farewell to the two women, slipped out. Lucy's whispered interrogations continued, cut off by the door I closed behind me.

CHAPTER 7

Mrs. Catt's hotel not being any great distance from the F Street office, I decided to enjoy the spring air and make my way there on foot. That season and the autumn are, the only times of year when my city is really welcoming to walkers, and I much preferred the colorful spectacle of a Washington D.C. crowd strolling amongst the blossoms to a solo journey. Years of perambulations upon these streets, coupled with Pierre Charles L'Enfant's celebrated urban design had left me quite at ease negotiating the Capital. This was particularly the case since I had no need to consider whether I strolled through the "good" portions of the city or the "bad."

I was wearing my glasses, and though I passed hundreds of people ambling singly or loitering in groups, I never experienced the shivering of reality that I'd come to associate with the presence of the Souls. This served to convince me that the creatures had not merely somehow become suddenly ubiquitous, but that their presence was indeed linked to the actions of Alice Paul's suffragists. I was more determined than ever to uncover an explanation.

Mrs. Catt greeted me at the door; resplendent in a rust-colored damask suit. It was clear she had been waiting for my knock. She appeared to be in her fifties, an attractive woman grown somewhat substantial with age, with her short, curled hair parted neatly in the middle. Her smile was full of bonhomie, but her distinctive, dark blue eyes were calculating. All told, she was far closer to the image that the public imagination held of the suffragist than was Alice Paul. This was a general misconception that I confess I had previously shared: a woman fierce, somewhat mannish, and aggressively political.

She had prepared tea in advance of my visit, and poured as I sat. I brought the cup to my lips, pretending to sip—an illusion that somehow never fails, as a result of the rituals surrounding this beverage—as she seated herself across from me.

"I want to thank you first, Mrs. Monot, for your generous contribution to our cause," she began.

Resettling my cup, and enjoying the tiny bell-like ring as bone china met its kin, I cast my eyes down and corrected her.

"It is Miss, please. I have not yet consented to matrimony."

She laughed softly, a girlish affectation that was jarringly false.

"Ah," she said, "forgive me. But a beauty like you must have suitors by the dozen."

I smiled at her, letting the sun catch my tinted lenses and briefly make mirrors of their surfaces.

"Fewer than you might think, Mrs. Catt. I've been given to understand that I can be a difficult woman."

"So have we all!" she said, quick to establish common ground. "It is a charge too commonly made against those of us who are willing to think for ourselves."

"And do you?" I asked, lifting the cup again briefly before resettling it.

"Do I what, Miss Monot?" Mrs. Catt sipped her own tea to punctuate the question.

"Do you always think for yourself, or do you at times turn to the spirit world for advice?"

The woman appeared genuinely puzzled by this question, but I had learned that those in politics are often as adept at acting as any of the stars of the stage.

"I believe your question is a generation too late, Miss Monot," she said. "Many of the early champions of our cause —such as the infamous Victoria Woodhull—professed belief in Spiritualism, but I think you'll find our movement has since been purged of such superstition. Surely a modern woman such as you does not cling to a belief in table-knocking?"

"I do so try to keep up with the times," I assured her, "but I also endeavor to maintain an open mind. Did not the Bard caution us that there are more things in heaven and earth than are dreamed of in our philosophy?"

Mrs. Catt studied me suspiciously, cunning apparent in her dark eyes.

"What exactly is the purpose of your visit, Miss Monot?" she asked.

"Curiosity, no more and no less," I assured her, dismissing suspicion with a languid wave. "Since becoming invested in the cause of suffrage, I have only encountered Alice Paul and her little coterie. I know the movement is not as young as its members appear to be, and wished to educate myself about its more established tenets."

"You are correct in thinking that Miss Paul is not representative of the whole of our cause. It might even be accurate to label her an outlier," she said. "But I can assure you that we—and even she—seek the vote rather than whispers from the otherworld. The suffragist of today is practical, hardworking, and able to take the long view. Our cause will not be won with miracles, but with persistence and a tireless effort across the years."

Aside from a tightening in the corners of her eyes when she was forced to say Alice's name, I saw no evidence of willful untruth in Carrie Catt's statement. She clearly had no love for the little suffragist, but just as plainly gave no hints suggesting an involvement with Spiritualism. I spent another twenty minutes in her company, discussing her hopes for the movement. She waxed warm about the prospects for several additional states passing suffrage legislation in the years ahead, before I politely took my leave.

As I was exiting the hotel, I found myself entertaining doubts about the entire enterprise. Why should I concern myself in a matter that offered me no benefit? As these misgivings continued to trouble me, I perceived a blur in the corner of my vision. Whipping my glasses from my eyes, I spied another of the Souls there.

It was a woman this time, but she fled upon being recognized and was gone before I could engage her in conversation. Gone just as quick were any doubts I'd had about my interest in such things. The creatures clearly wished that I would abandon my inquiries, which only strengthened my resolve to continue.

CHAPTER 8

Despite my determination to go forward with my investigation, it was some time before I returned to the F Street office. The recent appearance of Bryan Card, the Kin whose carelessness and greed had unintentionally lead to my making, continued to prey upon my thoughts. I conquered my aversion to the telephone long enough to contact several of my acquaintances among our Kind in order to assure myself allies should a confrontation with him prove unavoidable.

Many would consider this evidence of excessive caution on my part. Physical conflicts among the Kin are extremely rare. Why, after all, would one risk what is a virtual immortality in order to respond to anything less than the gravest provocation? Still, I knew that I might have to at least threaten Card to end his attentions, and after several telephone calls I was certain that I could do so if forced.

As I tallied my contacts, I realized that most of my close allegiances proved to be with female Kin. I had never before recognized that fact, and it was perhaps my dalliance with the suffragists that compelled me to view those relationships through the filter of gender. I did count Mark Reston of Kansas City among my closest associates, but my friendship with him only developed as a result of an earlier alliance with Mamie Clover, his partner in preeminence among the Midwestern Kin.

Mamie had been one of the first to advocate for me upon my unusual making. Though she had certainly been crucial to Lady Ellen Terry's championing of my cause, it would be difficult to imagine two women more different than the fabled actress who led London's Kin and this quintessential woman of the American West. Kansas City was the hub of Mamie's territory, but at the time it had yet to tally even a quarter million inhabitants. She had been shaped by the plains while warm, and changed little after her making. Plainspoken, honest, and true as a well-thrown blade, when she gave her allegiance, she did so without reservation and indelibly.

It was not unusual for a Master or Mistress of a city to have a companion, but in most cases such relationships were unequal, with the latter often being the creation of the former. Mamie and Mark were an exception to this rule, and managed their fiefdom as a partnership. Each brought his or her specific abilities to the task of managing the politics of the Kin in what was still unsettled land. I was not privy to the discussions that lead to the favorable resolution of my case, but was confident that the words of the Kansas contingent weighed heavily upon my side of the scales.

Mamie was aware of the circumstances of my making, but was far too circumspect to broach the subject with me directly. So when I informed her about my encounter with Bryan, she grasped the crux of the matter immediately

"It always troubles me to see the Gift go wasted," she said, "but if ever it was so it was with that one. He's been Kin longer than you. If he had your gumption, he'd be rich enough in his own right and wouldn't need to stoop so low. You just tell him to back off, Paulie, and you let him know in no uncertain terms that Mark and I stand by you on this."

"I appreciate that," I said, conscious of (and resisting) the urge to slip into a parody of her accent while talking to her. "It won't likely come to anything. He's not a fighter, but he does seem to have a talent for making trouble."

We made some small talk, and I promised to keep her abreast of the situation before ringing off, vaguely glad to be done with the infernal device. At the time, I was still uncomfortable with what seemed then a revolutionary technology. Speaking into the upright transmitter while hearing a living voice through the earpiece felt like a perversion of face-to-face conversation. I have, in general, been an enthusiastic adopter of the advances of science over the years, but I suppose we all stub our toes on innovation once in a while.

What with unanswered calls and callbacks, and the confusion of time zones, I spent entirely too much time in such unnatural conversations while metaphorically circling my wagons. So when I did finally turn my attention toward the suffragists again I suppose I should not have been surprised to discover matters somewhat changed.

First and foremost, they had relocated their offices to a large home made available by a wealthy supporter, a site I was aware of but had not yet visited. Alice stayed there now

(Lucy having found a hovel of her own), as did a rotating crew of willing volunteers. I was surprised to discover that there existed a veritable network of informed young women willing to involve themselves in the causes of the age; they were hungry for experience and fearless in many ways. It was also, perhaps more importantly, still within a slogan's shout of the president's front door.

Arriving there, I was fortunate enough to find Alice unoccupied. The spoor of recent activity surrounded her, however, in the form of piles of paper many inches high, their lower levels already showing a hint of discoloration and creasing at the edges where the stacks had been regularly straightened in an attempt to achieve at least the appearance of order, creating a sort of informational stratification. She peered up at me over one such pile, her striking eyes, as always, bright and challenging.

"Miss Monot," she said, acknowledging my presence, "it would seem that your visit to Mrs. Catt succeeded in provoking her to action, if nothing else."

"Really?" I asked. "For she appeared to be far more interested in my donation than anything I had to say. It was quite clear, however, that she bears you no little animosity, though I wouldn't hazard a guess as to its cause."

"Mrs. Catt grows older," she said, "and struggles with the weight of her years. She is forced to watch her husband noticing those who possess the beauty she has lost. That is often enough, sad though it might be, for a woman to develop animosity toward her younger sisters."

I feigned understanding, quietly thankful that I would never have to face such a test. "I think it difficult to find a movement salubrious that would consume its own young," I said.

She sniffed dismissively.

"When the torch is not passed, it must be snatched away," she said. "Mrs. Catt works ever harder to turn her Association's back on our efforts, and I shall not allow petty jealousy to stand in the way of our enfranchisement. Thus, Miss Burns and I have begun taking steps to separate our campaign from those of NAWSA. Let them continue their plodding efforts toward a state-by-state solution. Our new Congressional Union will spearhead the drive for an amendment to the Constitution which will win the vote for women across the nation in a single stroke." This was as close to an extemporaneous speech as I'd ever heard her venture, and she blushed at the outburst even as her gleaming eyes testified to her belief.

"Perhaps that is what your enemy truly fears," I said. "As Lucy posited, it could be that Carrie Catt cannot bear the thought that she has given her youth to the cause only to have the prize snatched away by a younger woman with a different strategy. Whatever the reason, however, I do suspect that the Souls who harass your movement owe something to that person's hatred." I glanced around the new office before continuing. "Where, by the way, is your redheaded partner in crime? Off haranguing the locals again, I presume?"

Alice pursed her lips, considering how to answer.

"I had to send her home to rest," she finally said. "She has been so very weary lately, and her attention suffers. As impulsive as Miss Burns is, I fear that in a compromised state, she might say or do something to the detriment of the cause."

This news interested me, and I went to some pains to disguise the level of my concern.

"How long has she been not herself?" I asked.

"For some days now," Alice said, "I thought obtaining a place of her own would benefit her, but as yet it seems to have had the opposite effect. I'm still hopeful that a decent amount of sleep will put her to rights again."

"I'm sure you're correct," I said, "but perhaps I should pay her a visit, if only to see if there are any errands I might run for her to allow her more time for recuperation."

Alice made no immediate reply, but her calculating gaze made it clear that she did not believe my motives were as innocent as I'd claimed. She did, however, scrawl an address on the corner ripped from one of the uppermost pages on the left-hand pile and passed it to me.

"Take care of her," she said. "I cannot do this alone. I need her back."

CHAPTER 9

If the location of the original suffragist office had not been prepossessing, the neighborhood surrounding Lucy's apartment was even less so. Her building squatted among factories and warehouses, demonstrating all the inviting ambiance of a cardboard box left some days at the mercy of the elements. The entryway stank of urine, and though her apartment was on the fourth floor, there was no elevator in the offing. The stairs were dark, narrow, and every third step seemed to move underfoot as if its boards had come loose of their moorings. The rent could not have been more than $7.50 a month, but it was clearly no bargain even at such a rate.

As I mounted the stairs, the reek of the entrance was gradually overwhelmed by cooking odors long absorbed into the woodwork and saturating the torn and bubbled wallpaper. The tenants here apparently lived on stewed things, primarily leaf vegetables and potatoes. The aroma also included the underlying metallic bite of organ meats, probably indulged in as a luxury.

Lucy had no reason to expect my visit, as I had taken no steps to alert her in advance. Before knocking on the door, I paused a few moments to compose myself, lest any visible concern prematurely alert her to the nature of my suspicions. When I felt myself mastered, I rapped sharply on the oft-painted wood.

I heard a muffled reply from within, but it was too indistinct for me to make out the words. No matter, for seconds later the door cracked open and Lucy Burns peered out at me through the narrow opening, and I knew at once that my worst fears were confirmed.

Rather than reveal these, I smiled and asked after her health, claiming that Alice Paul had bid me look in on her. Lucy returned my smile, though her expression was a beat too slow, as a daydreamer will always seem a step behind when trying to maintain a conversation. She opened the door wide, and I entered the apartment.

Her bright hair hung unbound, and she was garbed in a loose dressing gown of cotton so thin that the darker skin of her nipples showed through the cloth when a movement snugged it against her. The apartment was tiny and in great disarray. The bed was unmade and likely had been so for days. Every horizontal surface, including the arms of the lone stuffed chair, was stacked high with books, magazines, and assorted papers.

None of this particularly surprised me, as I was familiar with the orderly chaos of the suffragist's offices, and had even braved Ellen Terry's dressing room. More interesting to me was the faint lingering of a manly cologne in the air (a scent too familiar to me), the strange languor that infected

Lucy's manner, and the eerie translucency that now exaggerated her redhead's paleness.

"I'm not the first to visit you here," I said, glancing meaningfully at the tangle of sheets atop the narrow bed. Lucy glanced at me suspiciously upon this remark, its words seemingly penetrating the fog in which her mind was wrapped.

"I am an adult," she said, rather defensively, "and thus can entertain whom I wish without answering to anyone, including you, Miss Monot."

I adopted a conciliatory tone.

"Did I take you to task, Lucy dear? We are both women of the world. There is nothing you could confess, even were you moved to do so, that would shock me in the least."

This appeared to provide her comfort enough to allow her to reveal what she had clearly been desperate to share.

"It's true," she said, "I have a gentleman friend. The cause might be enough for dear Alice, but I am not made of such stern stuff. I have been so lonely, Paulette. Surely you understand the need to be appreciated, to be touched..."

"Oh, I do," I simpered, probing gently to draw out the truth entire. "But he does more than touch you, does he not?"

It was too much, and her suspicions flared anew.

"So you know," she said, backing away from me. "He may have been yours once, but he is mine now, and I will not let him return to you!"

It was in the open then, and all my worries confirmed. The time for our *pas de deux* of politesse was past.

"He was not my lover, Lucy Burns, but my murderer. And he would kill you while indulging in his own pleasure as casually as you would peel an orange." So saying, I made sure the door was pulled behind me and positioned myself between the redhead and that exit.

Lucy had clearly thought herself alone in knowing the great secret of her lover's nature, just as I had when as a mortal girl I had found myself with a Kindred paramour. My statement obviously shocked and confused her, but she was as yet unready to surrender her sense of uniqueness.

"You will not frighten me away with your lies, Paulette Monot. Are you not standing here in front of me as solid as any woman? Bryan did not harm anything but your pride. He threw you over, and now you seek a discarded mistress' revenge!"

I stepped forward and grasped her bare forearm. She gasped at the affront and attempted to pull free, but I held her firm.

"I am solid, yes, Lucy dear," I said, "but my flesh is cold, is it not? Even like his own? And I am far stronger than you imagined a spoiled rich girl such as I might be. Will you not remove the blinders that you wear and dare to gaze at the world as it is?"

I watched the progress of realization in her eyes, as anger turned to fear, and fear to wonder.

"You are what he is. Did Bryan make you so?" She whispered this, no longer struggling against my grasp.

"Your creature had not a thought of turning me into what I am. He drank from and discarded my mortal body as a libertine will drain a cup and toss it over his shoulder. It was only by the purest chance that another's blood found its way to my lips and remade me. If not, I should have been just another corpse found alone in her room, for the police to forget about and the public to bury." The accidental nature of my making rankled anew; and having revealed it I felt no compulsion to further confess that the blood that had transformed me was weaker than that of her swain.

"I am quite wealthy," I continued, "and the creature who enthralls you would claim some of those riches for his own, as I believe you might have overhead. He noted my involvement with the cause championed by you and Miss Paul, and all but assured me that he would prey upon my affection for you two in order to force my hand. He has no love for you, Lucy; you are no more to him than a means to an end."

"But surely you know what it is like, when he...when he takes my blood." She cast her eyes down as she spoke. "I have never imagined such ecstasy, and I believe I might die were I forced to do without it."

"Silly girl!" I said, gripping her arm again, this time so fiercely that she cried out in pain. "Do you not see that one day soon he will prolong that pleasure recklessly, and when there is nothing more for him to take, you will be left on this floor with your heart stopped, bereft of all life and all pleasure forever more?"

She wailed at this declaration.

"Even if what you say is true," she forced out the words between sobs, "I don't believe I could resist. How am I to go back to being the lonely little dog's body suffragist that I was, when I have known a pleasure that leaves my mind with no room for anything but sensation? Surely no opiate ever ensnared its user more completely than this ecstasy has made me its slave."

She was shivering with emotion by then, and I captured her other arm to steady her as I struggled with my reply.

CHAPTER 10

Lucy was not at her best; her eyes red with weeping and her face clenched with it, teardrops darkening spots on her thin cotton robe. So I cannot contend that I was overcome with desire, or that anything other than a wish to counter my enemy drove me to do what I did.

"He is not the sole purveyor of that narcotic, dear Lucy," I said, lifting my chin to look up at her through the filters of my tinted lenses.

She blinked, and surely would have rubbed her eyes had I not still kept her arms imprisoned. She answered in a small voice and drew her head back as she did so in a gesture of futile retreat.

"What do you mean?" she said.

I was surprised at her question, for I knew her to be a quick-witted girl and had thought my statement quite self-explanatory. Still, I assumed that the fog of lust she labored through had clouded her thoughts. Clearly something had to be done. Again I hesitated, knowing that unless I enchanted her, which I was loath to do, there would be no retreating from the step I contemplated. And enchanting her would leave her with no memory of what followed, and thus have no real benefit. As I waffled, I saw Bryan's leering face in my mind's eye, and wanted only to strike at it.

"I'm sure he has told you nothing," I said, "since he mistakes obfuscation for subtlety. We call ourselves Kin. I say 'we' because I am as much so as he."

Here, I loosened my grip on her bare arms and stroked the hollows of her elbows with my thumbs. "Whatever pleasure you've found when he feeds upon you can also be found with me, and I would offer it with real affection and a promise that you will not be harmed."

Her hands caught my arms and she stepped closer. I could feel the warmth of her skin filling the space between us; hear the gradual quickening of her breath.

She stared down at my face. Her features visibly softened, and her voice crept out on a whisper.

"Are you saying that you want to have your way with me, Paulette?" she asked.

The die cast, I favored her with a tart smile.

"*With* you, Lucy dear, I assure you I will expect full reciprocity. But only if I have your word that you will no longer entertain the despicable Mr. Card."

In answer, she glanced at the tangled bed. My sense of smell was keen enough to know that it contained evidence of previous passions, both hers and my enemy's, but I have never been overly fastidious, and determined then and there to accept the challenge of that trysting spot and erase his memory with my own. I freed my right arm from hers and let my left hand slide down her skin until it clasped her right.

We reached the twisted sheets without another word being spoken.

Standing there I paused, releasing her hand and placing both of mine upon her hips. I allowed our bodies to find their proper meshing; hers naked beneath the thin veil of cotton, mine still armored in the fashion of the day.

"Promise me," I said, chin tilted up and my eyes still shielded; my face close enough to hers for her to feel the breeze of the words upon her own lips.

"I am yours!" she sighed, and fell to the bed as if in a swoon.

I could not help but notice that she landed artfully enough to display her curves to good effect, even uncovering one leg to just above the knee. If Lucy thought to ignite the predator in me with this vulnerable melodrama, I was determined to show her that Paulette Monot is not so easily manipulated.

Those who are aware of my history will know that I am a woman of catholic appetite, but rather than fall upon the girl and rip the gown from her with impatient hands, I set to deliberately disrobing myself. My personal history had left me confident of the allure of my form, though it might not be as voluptuous as the current fashion proscribes. I revealed it with deliberate care, folding garments neatly as I discarded them, and stretching to celebrate the liberation of the skin beneath.

I was aware that, far from being lost to fainting, Lucy followed my every step with eager eyes. When I had shed all but a silken camisole and knicker set, and was thus more nearly naked than she, I approached the bed. Hands on the sheets, I leaned toward her, knowing full well the show this made of my bosom.

"I know you want to touch me." I fairly hissed the words. "Here, I'll even help you." With that I lifted her arm, she still feigning limpness, until the weight of my right breast was fairly cupped in the palm of her hand. This was all it took to break my redhead's pretended reticence. She lunged forward and fairly dragged me onto the bed, her mouth questing and hungry upon my own.

I could not tell you how we removed her gown and my underthings, only that it was done with urgency and without any of the awkward capture of limbs that such undressings are prone to. In moments, we were both fully unclothed. With Lucy's surrender to her own desire evidenced, I was ready to lead our dance.

We kissed; her mouth hot and mine chill, our tongues and lips and teeth busy with love's devouring. I maneuvered her easily until I was beside her and she on her back; and set out to purge all memory of Bryan from her mind and body.

There is no need to detail our lovemaking here. Suffice it to say that by the time my teeth slipped into her in that most intimate of penetrations my mouth and hands had twice drawn the bow of her body tight and twice released it. I supped only daintily, knowing that another had already weakened her. Nevertheless, Lucy reveled fully in the ecstasy of the feeding, her twin journeys to orgasm priming her for this greater pleasure. When we were finished, she clung to me, limp and warm and moist from her exertions, as if she could never bear to release me.

CHAPTER II

Though the amorously besotted often claim they would abandon all for love, precious few do so. And so I eventually reassembled my accouterment and, with many a kiss and promise to repeat our pleasures soon, left Lucy Burns' apartment and returned to the greater world. I was not naïve enough to believe that I had vanquished my rival with one engagement, but however much I despised Bryan and hoped to return Lucy to a productive efficiency, there were numerous other matters still upon my plate.

Much of my time was still spent arranging the metaphorical scented candles and soft music intended to put my wealth in the mood to reproduce. Like an avaricious mother setting a trap for a prosperous son-in-law, I perhaps indulged in this stage-setting overmuch. Couple that obsessive behavior with an immortal's casual approach to time, and it will be no surprise that the attention I paid to the cause of suffrage was far from constant.

Oh, I did honor my monthly financial pledge; indeed, I had arranged matters with my bank so that it could be done without any action on my part. And I did, for long enough it seems, maintain my physical relationship with Lucy. There was no love in those dalliances, and it happened that even the narcotic of the feeding lost some of its hold upon the girl after a long familiarity. Worse yet, I realized in the middle of a particularly intimate act of love that I was more performer than participant.

So when I discovered that she had taken a male paramour, presumably mortal, I was almost grateful to grant her freedom from my attentions.

There were others, however, who took the long view just as I did, and the fact that I had not again encountered them had not signaled an end to their activities.

This became clear to me when I eventually did revisit the suffragists' offices. As I approached the front door I noted the now familiar blurring at the edge of my vision, and slipped off my glasses to spot a trio of Souls fleeing my attention. I pursued them briefly, only to lose sight of them on the busy sidewalks, and so returned to the suffragists' building with some trepidation.

The atmosphere when I entered could be likened to that of a rainy day that had just surrendered to sunshine. Alice Paul was standing, clearly furious, and the three women whom she had obviously been haranguing looked at her all befuddled, as if just awakened from a dream. The little brunette glanced up at my entry and greeted me wryly.

"So it is you, and they've fled from your spying eyes. I would that you were here always, Miss Monot. I might find my staff more productive if you were." I immediately surmised that the Souls whom I'd seen had been spreading their signature poison among those working in the office.

"And how is it that the baneful influence does not extend to you, Alice?" I said. "Furthermore, since you can see the creatures as well as I, why do they not fly before you?" It was dangerous to speak so plainly in front of the company, but I fancied that the workers would be too busy recovering their wits to take notice. Alice was not as reckless as I, and led me into her tiny office before continuing the discussion.

When we had entered and the door was shut behind us, she continued.

"As to your questions, I can only hazard guesses. Perhaps I am immune to their influence by virtue of my ability to see them. That alone gives me no power over them, however, and it could be that there is some way that you can harm them, albeit as yet unknown to you."

"If I discover such, I can assure you that I will take great pleasure in employing it," I said. "But the so-called Souls were focusing their efforts on the opponents of your organization when I was here last. How have they come to be spreading their doubts among your own staff?"

Alice glanced at the closed door, as if she worried that some sort of insurrection might be brewing beyond it.

"They appear to be stronger, or at the least more numerous," she said, "and their success among Mrs. Catt's supporters has been such that we have been forced to break all ties with NAWSA. Miss Burns and I now lead The Woman's Party from these august chambers, and still hope to appeal directly to the voters as did the suffragists of a generation ago."

"But she is not here?" I asked.

Alice studied me, and though I seldom respect a mortal's gaze, I felt the shrewdness in those strange, violet eyes.

"Miss Burns is out of the office at present, but I find her condition much improved. I suppose I have you to thank for that as well; at least she no longer moons about doodling your name as she did some months back."

I allowed myself a blush. Though I felt no shame, I had found it a useful reaction to mimic, and practiced it when it seemed appropriate.

"I trust the friendship between Lucy and me is undiminished," I said, "but only entering another stage."

Alice huffed through her nose in derision.

"Well, I'm glad to have her back, regardless of the reason," she said. "I've long since forced myself to accept that Miss Burns cannot muster the single-minded devotion to our cause that I feel."

"Such a focused dedication can be dangerous, Alice, like a cart driven at speed without concern for whatever else might share the street."

The suffragist stiffened.

"I did not, I believe, ask your advice, Miss Monot. And I have an intimate knowledge of the sort of roadblocks that are continually put in our way. Our travel has been anything but speedy, as you well know."

"It would seem to me," I said, "that the self-named 'Souls' are the most significant barrier you face at the moment. Perhaps we should focus our attentions there?"

"'We,' Miss Monot? We? You drop by here will-I-nil-I, apparently on little more than your own whims, and I am to abandon everything in order to attend to the matter you consider most pressing? Perhaps you think that you should be leading the Woman's Party rather than me? Shall I just step aside and offer you my chair?" Here, she actually did rise from her seat behind the desk and made as if to leave it.

I applauded her sense of drama, which I think only infuriated her more.

"As you well know, Alice"—childish though it was, how I enjoyed figuratively poking the finger of her given name into her angry violet eye—a "I am immune to your persecutions, and little more than curious about your movement. I fear it would all fall asunder under my negligent leadership. Consider my words as advice offered, rather than action demanded, and perhaps we can accomplish something together?"

She did not rise to the bait of my use of her first name, but rather accepted my point gracefully.

"The Souls then, Miss Monot," she said (this use so automatic to her that I doubted it was an intended dig), "how do you propose we deal with them?"

I confess I had no ready answer, and was prepared to admit this when the door opened and Lucy Burns walked in.

She was flushed from hurry, her lush red hair in some disarray, but I was pleased to note that the girl appeared to be healthy and, on the surface at least, happy. Still, she was unable to control a blush at finding me there, and addressed me cautiously.

"Paulette," she said, "how nice to see you again."

I was quick to disabuse her of any thoughts that I might harbor resentment over the end of our brief affair.

"Lucy!" I said, with some enthusiasm not altogether false. "You look lovelier than ever. Would I be correct in assuming that you've brought your personal and professional lives into a satisfactory balance?"

Her relief was obvious, as was Alice's clinical study of our little interchange.

"What Miss Burns considers a fair balance, I find weighted heavily in favor of the personal," she said, "but I suppose suffrage should be grateful for whatever crumbs she can spare it."

Lucy was not intimidated.

"We can't all be saints, Alice," she replied, "and I'd wager a bit of the old slap and tickle would work wonders for your management style. In case you hadn't noticed, there's a good bit of trouble in our ranks."

"I am not prepared, I think, to shoulder all of the blame for that," the brunette replied. "But perhaps your friend, Miss Monot, will be able to aid us."

I was not oblivious to the ice with which Alice encased the word "friend," but perhaps I was less cognizant of the impact that Lucy's admonition had upon her. If I had recognized that warning, I might have been better prepared for what was to come.

CHAPTER 12

One might think that a person, suddenly gifted with the opportunity to taste immortality, would embrace that miracle by scrubbing him or herself of the imperfections accumulated over the course of a mortal life. Sadly, most of us (and I include myself among that number) merely continue much as we were, allowing the passage of years to set such stains ever more indelibly into our characters.

Such was certainly the case with Bryan Card. By all accounts a rake and a bounder when warm, he had apparently counted his Kindred powers as little more than the means to more widely indulge his appetites, and to do so with less concern for their impacts upon those he victimized. Thus, while I, and many others of my Kind, would consider using our powers of Entrancement as means to a seduction poor form at best, he apparently had no such misgivings.

He had made attempts to re-ensnare Lucy Burns, but found her first besotted with yours truly, and later weaned of her addiction to the blood feed. He spent little time in mourning her loss and turned his attentions elsewhere. He was also, I fear, the type who takes a perverse satisfaction in the ruin of the most resolute. In short, I should have been able to predict his next move, and might have been able to more effectively counter it had I done so.

As ever, my involvement with the suffragists was in no manner constant. The only regular contact I maintained was the automatic donations that accounted for an ever more insignificant depletion of my fortune as the latter accumulated. Thus, the occasion of my next visit to their headquarters was marked with twin surprises.

In the first place, I encountered no sign of the Souls in the vicinity neither in their characteristic blurring of the edge of my vision while my lenses were in place, nor in their more apparent form when I removed those filters, which I assuredly did for a cautious glance around before entering the establishment.

More puzzling still, I found the atmosphere in the outer office dramatically changed. Where previously the young women were one and all busily proselytizing on telephones or pecking furiously at typewriters, when I entered I found them clustered together. Some were sitting on the edge of a desk, chatting happily. Strangest of all, the door to Alice Paul's inner sanctum was tightly closed. When I went to open it, one of the girls interrupted her gossip long enough to tell me that "the boss" was not to be disturbed.

Put it down to arrogance, but I've typically assumed that such rules do not pertain to me. So I tried the knob, found the door locked, and knocked. When no reply was forthcoming (though I knew someone was within, for an empty room can clearly be felt to be such from without) I rapped more forcefully. This also elicited no response, however. I decided that—arrogant or not—breaking in the door to gain admission would be a clear violation, given the roomful of witnesses who regarded my actions with growing horror.

Perhaps I was feeling petulant, for I am not immune to such indulgences. At any rate, I withered the office girls with a glance that effectively stifled any comments about my presumption in assaulting the locked door, and made my way out with an air of royalty wronged, only to almost collide with Lucy Burns at the entrance to the flat.

The redhead, clearly agitated, glanced from me to the locked inner door and sighed.

"Ah, so you know then," she said.

"I know nothing, Lucy," I replied. "Perhaps you'd be kind enough to enlighten me?"

The woman glanced at the closed office, and at the curious audience watching our interaction before—with a boldness that surprised me—grasping my hand and fairly dragging me out into the street.

Once beyond the doors, she rounded on me with exasperation.

"Are you being purposefully obtuse, Paulette?" she began, hands on her hips. "For I think I know some little bit of the capabilities of your mind, and you most certainly must be able to intuit what has happened."

She was certainly correct, but even the Kin are not immune to that human penchant of choosing not to see what they dread, though the evidence is clearly before them. Thus, rather than admit to the thought that was even then worming into my mind, I pushed her again.

"I fear I must bow to your wisdom in this matter, my dear," I said, "and wait for your elucidation."

The redhead stamped a foot in frustration. Despite my unease, I could not help but admire the reverberations of that action as they reached the full breasts to which I had paid ample attention.

"It is he!" she cried. "He has reached her and she is under his spell, even as I was!"

It was as if a shade had been lifted from mind, and that which I knew but was loath to admit revealed itself in sudden clarity. I felt rush of anger, hot and pure.

"Alice Paul did not allow this willingly," I said. "She is not as you are." I added, perhaps out of kindness, "Or as I was once."

Though my words could be construed as insult, Lucy took them without umbrage.

"What will you do, Paulette?"

I confess I was somewhat taken aback by the faith implied by those few words.

"I will stop him," I said, with a confidence that I didn't feel. "It is me that he strikes at through Alice, and that impertinence I cannot let stand."

CHAPTER 13

If my pledge was made in haste, I allowed myself some leisure to contemplate its fulfillment. Though each day lost to Alice was sand forever relegated to the bottom of her hourglass (and that of her cause), my enemy and I existed at a slower pace, and haste would not, I presumed, necessarily result in the wisest of decisions.

It was also possible, I conjectured, that by not immediately responding I could cause him to assume that his conquest of the little brunette had not irked me as he'd hoped. If this were the case, Card might abandon those efforts (and thus free Alice from his attentions) in order to contemplate a more telling assault, or simply attempt to do away with her Should either of these occur, I was still determined to counter him, but would hope do so with less risk of trauma to the suffragist.

I must also mention that events on the international scale provided me with a good bit of distraction. The assassination of Austria's Archduke Ferdinand by a Bosnian Serb set off a veritable domino fall of treaties made and broken and declarations of war. Under the tutelage of Cecil Rhodes, I had learned that military hostilities often created a petri dish in which wealth can thrive, but only if one's investments were agile enough to anticipate and counter the contrariness of nations. The burgeoning war kept me on my toes financially, though at the time I could not foresee the ramifications that the growth of militancy would have for Alice Paul and her compatriots.

The little brunette's bullheadedness itself proved a revelation as well. For though her effectiveness as a leader was certainly compromised by my enemy's attentions, even he was incapable of tempting her to remove her shoulder from the plow. Though perhaps not with the resolution it might otherwise have enjoyed, the struggle for suffrage blundered forward.

It is also likely that Lucy Burns (frustrated, I'm sure, by my lack of immediate action) picked up some of the slack left by her Entranced captain. Regardless, as the world became day-by-day more embroiled in apocalypse, a series of broadsides continually reminded the American public (whose nation so far managed to sit firmly on the sidelines) that while the planet embarked upon a huge struggle for liberty, fully half of the population of the self-proclaimed "land of the free" was still without a vote.

For the moment satisfied that Card's intervention would not sink the suffragists, I was able to return my attention to my investments. As I have said, if war creates a situation friendly to the growth of wealth, it also can prove difficult to navigate. Soon after the commencement of hostilities, Britain and her allies established a naval blockade effectively preventing commerce with Germany and Austria. Though my French ancestry tended to swing my sympathies toward that nation and her English allies,), this complicated the management of my money.

Germany in particular was hungry for goods to which I had access, and the U.S. being neutral, I found myself frustrated to be locked out of that profitable trade. For a time, I was able to circumvent the blockades by working through intermediaries in Sweden. This use of a middleman certainly cut into my profits, but fortunately these were substantial enough to allow me to happily absorb the resulting fees. However, the British and French uncovered this ruse in short order, and countered it by extending their blockades to include even the European neutrals. I was able to maintain the levels of my trade with little interruption, but I found myself doing business with entities that required more time than my established customers.

Rhodes had taught me that currency knows no nation and is quite devoid of emotion. I struggled to remember this as my maneuvers were time and again frustrated and I was forced to jink and swerve like a hunted fox. More than once, I wished I could telephone the financier and enjoy the calming influence of his little voice that so belied the bull-like nature of the man, but could not. He had some years since died or disappeared, and I was effectively on my own.

Thankfully, I had my own experiences to guide me. Both the Matabele War and the Boxer Uprising had taught me that, more than fabrics and oil, armies require starch and steel. They fuel their bodies with the former, and pierce those of their enemies with the latter, so it was in these two areas that I concentrated my investments.

American Blood

As the conflict progressed, other developments came into play. Unable to match the traditional seagoing power of the British, Germany turned more and more toward their new submarines, the so-called *unterseebooten,* to counter blockade measures. Many considered this an unnatural form of warfare (though the combatants one and all were happy to employ other measures that were, to my eyes, at least as distressing). When one of these stealthy vessels sank the *Lusitania,* causing the loss of more than one hundred American lives, the drumbeat for war on this side of the Big Pond became increasingly louder.

President Wilson had no choice but to respond angrily to this maritime tragedy. The Germans waxed conciliatory, pledging to warn any American ships attempting to provide solace to the allies before firing upon them, and to rescue passengers should hostilities prove unavoidable. To my mind, the writing was on the wall, and I began to maneuver my investments in anticipation of America's entry into the war.

The changing political climate began to affect the impact of my pet suffragists as well. Though Lucy continued to crank out broadsides bemoaning the inconsistencies inherent in America's treatment of her gender, she lacked the nimble political mind of Alice Paul. Meanwhile, the national press relentlessly covered supposed wartime atrocities with the energy and invective it had once directed at the suffragist's tormentors. Thus, eventually Lucy's efforts proved stale, and the struggle for the vote was more and more relegated to the status of sideshow, tolerated or (perhaps worse) ignored.

I also turned a blind eye on these developments as long as I was able. The women's movement was, after all little more than a hobby for me. The virtual absence of the Souls convinced me that who or whatever was behind their meddling thought the battle won. To my mind only Bryan Card's efforts could have produced such confidence. So I regretfully turned my investments over to hands that I secretly believed were less competent than mine, and determined to take action.

CHAPTER 14

I could not employ the same tactics I had used to free Lucy Burns from my enemy's thrall. Alice had shown no interest in my considerable charms, and had I entranced her in order to control her affections she would be no more effective under my influence than she had proven to be under Card's. No, as much as the thought filled me with trepidation, only direct action would produce the results I hoped for.

I had laid the groundwork for such an effort already, and so after forcing myself once more to endure the magic of the long-distance telephone call, I arranged for Mamie Clover to visit my D.C. lodgings. Though this new technology allowed that conversation to be the work of minutes, travel was still a tedious affair. Thus, it was some days before my friend, who was forced to make the journey by rail and see to matters of protection from excessive daylight and her own sustenance during the trip, arrived in Washington.

It was her first sojourn this far east, and the hurry and bustle of my cosmopolitan home proved overwhelming to this lady of the Wild West at first. Thus, I sought to ease her introduction to urban ways. For the first few days, I kept her protected in my lodgings, and arranged for her to feed lightly and discretely upon such denizens of the demimonde, mostly ladies of the evening, as I could safely enthrall and lead back to our fortress. Soon, Mamie declared herself quite acclimated, and we began to plan in earnest.

We did so, being civilized modern women, over a mid-afternoon "tea." We were quite shielded from the insults of the sun, my shades and curtains drawn tight. Our biscuit, if you will, was a young doxy I had encountered in the waning hours of the evening, when she had been "working" for some time. Exhaustion and the lingering effects of various chemicals made her very susceptible to Entrancement. In that state I led her to my rooms and allowed her a few hours of precious sleep before her services were called for.

When awakened, she proved still quite amenable to suggestion, and I bade her sit between us at my dining room table. The girl (for she was certainly not out of her teens) was none too clean, and fairly reeked of her evening's employment, but the Kin, though our sense of smell is extremely sharp, and not overly fastidious about odor, and Mamie and I found her quite acceptable.

Though she was comely, we did not order her undressing (we are not monsters after all!), and merely sipped lazily from her two wrists as we plotted our offensive. At one point, my companion remarked upon a particular nuance of flavor which was unfamiliar to her. I opined that it was perhaps a residue of cocaine, which the girl had likely imbibed in order to manage the long hours her occupation demanded. This drug had perhaps not yet become widely available on the Frontier.

"Thus, we interspersed idle chatter with weightier matters as we enjoyed our "tea"—who had given her name as Coco, though that was almost certainly a *nom de nuit*. After we had finished, the girl was led to our front door and released from Enchantment and into the sunlight; weary, with her memory washed cleaner than her body, and her purse considerably heavier than she usually found it in morning. Mamie and I had dined only sparingly (it was a social occasion rather than a meal, after all), and returned to table alert and able to linger over the details of our plan of action. Bryan Card's personality, and indeed his campaign against me as manifested in the Entrancement of Alice Paul, had long been defined by greed, thus it was an easy decision to use this hunger to bait him. We had only to lure him to a site that provided a degree of isolation and to let him there discover that he faced not only Paulette Monot (who, though it irks me to say it, he had little to fear from) but the far more formidable Mamie Clover as well, and there to mete upon him punitive measures fitting his misdeeds.

It was also clear that his punishment must be terminal in nature. Card had been chased down and disciplined before for his part in making me, but as yet showed no inclination to cleave to the standards of decency accepted by the Kin. I understood this, but the thought of causing an end to another immortal creature gave me pause. I had only done so once before, and it was an event I was unable to recall

without distress.

It had been in London when, though at the conclusion of the first mission Lady Ellen Terry had charged me with, I was still far newer to the ways of the Kin than I am today. While hunting the back-alleys of that great city and reveling in the speed and silence proffered by my Horace-Wilkershire Coilcycle (the elegant spring-powered conveyance I had then rejoiced in owning), I had tracked what I thought to be a mortal ne'er do well, and perhaps one with murderous intent.

In retrospect, I should have been able to deduce his nature from the fluidity of his movements. But I was young and excited by the chase, so failed to note what would otherwise have been obvious clues. When I had slipped away from my vehicle and pounced upon him, it was immediately apparent that he not only shared my nature, but exceeded me in age and strength.

He proved as avaricious as Card, however, and I lured him to my lodgings with a promise of compensation. There, while he luxuriated in the novelty of indoor plumbing in my bath, I was able to take him by surprise and behead him with a length of piano wire. I fled England soon thereafter and never learned if his murder had been discovered by the Lady, but I had vivid memories of the bathwater darkening red as his head toppled into it. I still feared what repercussions I might face were my crime to be discovered.

When needs must the devil drives, so I put such worries behind me and, with Mamie's steadfast support, carried forward with our plan. The first difficulty was contacting Card, since I knew not his address. I could, I suppose, have simply accosted him going to or from one of his rendezvous with Alice Paul, but I hoped to keep the little suffragist distant from these proceedings, in part because I had no wish to later find that Card had brought her with him to our eventual assignation as insurance.

Though a woman of the Wild Frontier, Mamie Clover proved to be far more comfortable with modern technologies than I, and solved this problem soon enough. In the past, I have sometimes rushed forth in anger, and through luck or sheer stubbornness have so far survived such actions. Each has taught me something, and I was not inclined to beard Bryan Card without first preparing for the encounter in such a way that my success was at least as likely as my failure.

When all was in readiness, I steeled myself and called my enemy early one evening. He answered rapidly and, after hearing my proposal, pronounced himself glad that I had come to my senses and assured me that, once rewarded as he so rightly deserved, he would be quite happy to cut the little suffragist free, he having become rather bored with her, truth be told. Boredom would soon, I silently promised myself, be the least of his worries.

CHAPTER 15

After some negotiation (for he was cautious), we arranged to meet at a given point on the banks of the Potomac, far from factories and their prying eyes. Mamie would proceed in advance, and secret herself in the vicinity until her time came. Fortunately, I had in my possession a map of the city and bade her study it carefully, her knowledge of its layout being rudimentary at best. When she and I were both confident of her ability to reach the point of assignation, I sent her off in a horse cab, intending to follow later in order to arrive just in advance of our adversary.

Waiting did not suit my nature, but I had learned through hard teaching that time is, on occasion, the one ingredient that cannot be scrimped upon. As much as I might have chafed with waiting, wait I did, for the success of my enterprise, and indeed my own continued existence, might well depend upon the adhesive of the trap I had constructed setting fully before it was sprung.

Time is never a constant thing. The reader will understand how slowly the clock seemed to progress, its hand figuratively sawing through minutes as if each were as hard as ironwood. One would think that, with immortality in the offing, such small units of temporal measure would slip by almost unnoticed, but I assure you that even a theoretically endless supply of hours does nothing to speed the sixty minutes that lie between one and an anticipated event.

Though labored in its movement, the hour eventually passed (I did change my outfit twice in the interim, in a failed gambit to hurry it along), and I set out to the designated place of meeting. I also chose to travel by cab, and had the driver deposit me some blocks away from my ultimate destination, trusting that Mamie was already secreted nearby. It was dark, the site distant from the nearest streetlight. The air was redolent of the river, a noisone mixture of brackish water, fish, and rot. Choosing a position where Kindred eyes could not fail to see me silhouetted against the weak reflection of moonlight and river, I awaited Card's arrival.

Although I knew my enemy was older and more powerful than I—as Mistress of Washington D.C., I was perhaps more respected than he, but I owed that distinction to my fortune and Lady Terry's influence—it was still irritating to have him suddenly appear without my having noted his approach. I did not give vent to my surprise, but turned to him as if his presence were anticipated and foreseen.

He was, and I do not wish to belabor the point, quite beautiful. Tall and slender, and appearing to be near thirty years of age, he wore his hair longer than the current fashion and occasionally drew his hand over it as if petting a sleeping cat. He wore a dark wool frock coat over a black cherry

Jacquard vest and Thurston striped trousers, all cut to display his slim figure to good effect. His eyes were blue, and I was able to meet these fearlessly by virtue of the tinted glasses that I wore.

Card circled me lazily, his black lace-ups almost silent on the sandy soil here almost bereft of weed, and subjected me to a study that was as infuriating as it was impertinent. Having as yet detected no sign of Mamie, I was glad to let his little drama play out and wait for his opening salvo in order to allow more time for this key component to materialize.

"Oh, "he finally remarked, "you have become quite the little sensation, haven't you? An accident, a blow-by, and yet with a fiefdom all your very own while I can barely keep myself in clothes befitting my station. Well, we shall put those matters back in balance, shan't we? I'm sure you know you won't buy back your little playmate cheaply."

He was clearly unaware of the peculiar ability of tinted glasses to disguise the potency of the wearer's eyes, so I did have that card hidden in my hand. It was a weak one, and I again attempted to scan our surroundings for signs of the hidden Mamie Clover without alerting him.

As I did this I spoke, keeping my voice frosty.

"I recognize that you seek to improve your social status through blackmail," I said. "Rather than judge the appropriateness of such an approach, I would sooner have it done and be gone with you. How much will you ask to leave Alice Paul be and assure me that I shall never have the displeasure of your company again?"

He stopped in front of me, and made bold to chuck me beneath the chin with an affectionate knuckle.

"There is such authority in your voice, dear girl! I must remind myself that when first we met you were not at your best!" He smiled at me before continuing. "But I see I need to clarify matters. The payment you will make today will buy freedom for the little brunette. However, should I, say, any point in the future require additional funds, I will expect you to provide them. What choice do you have, after all? You cannot best me in a contest, and though you enjoy elevated status, I doubt you would want to call the attention of your betters to the corners they were forced to cut in establishing you as they did.

"No," he continued, his voice silky, "I'm afraid we are entering into a long term relationship. But what matter? You will never be poor, as you've shown an unlikely knack for making money. We are merely assuring that I will never be so, either. You, sweet Paulette, are to be my bank, to draw upon as needed."

I could scarcely bear his touch, and the further affront of his words was almost more than I could stand. Still, I saw no sign of Mamie anywhere in our vicinity, so I continued to delay, first taking a step back to discourage any further contact.

"That was not the arrangement I anticipated based on our earlier interaction." I said. "You implied to me that a single payment, which I am resigned will be exorbitant, would be enough to close all of our accounts. Why should I pay you now only to spend my nights ever after wondering when you might come back for more?"

He laughed at that, a delighted little chuckle punctuated by another stroke of his pelt of hair.

"But Paulette, *dear* Paulette," he said, "surely you recognize that you have no alternative. As much as I've found the little suffragist to be a bit of a cold fish, I am quite determined to maintain my hold on her until you've met my demands. What else can you do?" The more he spoke of my apparent helplessness, the more the notion seemed to arouse him.

There was still no sign of Mamie Clover. I feared that, despite the map, negotiating the streets of the city had proved too much for her and that she had either misdirected her cab or lost her way upon abandoning that vehicle. My patience was wearing thin, and I feared that Card would soon tire of the senseless negotiation and back his demands with action. Still, I resolved to delay while I could.

"You've proven to me that your word is worthless," I said, drawing out a brief document I'd prepared in advance. "But I still hold out some faint hope for the value of your signature. This paper states that, upon payment of the sum demanded, you will abandon all claims against me and mine. Tell me what you require, and I shall pay it in exchange for your name upon this page. Then, should your greed swell up again in the future, I will at least have something to present to our betters in my defense."

"You begin to bore me, Paulette," he replied, snatching the single sheet of foolscap from my hand with a show of speed that shocked me. He released it to flutter into the dark waters below. "Write me a chit for five thousand dollars now, with no guarantees binding me, or I will kill your little pet and let her movement flounder without her." I knew this was little more than feint and parry on his part. Card knew well enough that, though I had affection for the suffragists, I would sacrifice them on the altar of my own wellbeing without a thought.

He attempted to dominate me then, unaware of the prophylactic provided by my eyeglasses. Even with the protection of those tinted lenses I could feel the fingers of his power scrabbling at my will. I broke his gaze with no little effort, and cast a final futile glance around in search of Mamie Clover. Apparently I had no choice but to attempt action on my own.

"You leave me no options, it seems," I said, pretending to fish in my purse for a bank cheque as if his efforts to Entrance me had succeeded. "If I have no choice but to take your word, I suppose I must do so."

I watched the satisfaction creep over his lovely face. When I assumed him to be quite distracted with self-congratulation, I summoned all of the speed in my changed body and drove my hooked fingers at his unprotected eyes.

CHAPTER 16

It was as if I moved through water and he through air. With a nonchalance that hurt far worse than his grip, Card caught my hand mere inches from his face and snapped the bones of my wrist with a twist of his fingers and throwing me to the ground in a single motion.

I struggled with real fear now, as his anger was clearly aroused and my premature demise was a very clear possibility. Though I twisted with all my strength, stirring the damp sand around me with my efforts, he soon had me pinned under him. He seated himself on my chest with my arms beneath his knees.

"Silly girl," he lisped, his teeth arisen, "now you'll pay me in a richer coin, and get nothing at all in return."

I knew then that he intended to feed upon me, and in all likelihood dispatch me thereafter and consign my body to the Potomac. I had not been so pierced since my own change, and I am embarrassed to say that, even in the face of my own destruction, a part of me remembered the unmatched pleasure I had enjoyed in such co-mingling when warm, and wondered how it might be enhanced by my heightened senses.

In that mood, I ceased my struggles, and may even have turned my head to the side to allow him access. Those who have followed my history will know that I have never been what one might call a submissive woman, but it must be recognized that I was completely overmatched and that I have ever been susceptible to the whisperings of pleasure.

It was not to be, however; for even as he lowered his mouth to my neck—slowly so as to prolong the experience of his conquest—Card was struck from atop me and sent sprawling to the very edge of the river.

It was Mamie Clover, who, having departed her cab in the wrong location, had been scouring the banks since and come upon us at the most opportune moment.

She pulled me to my feet with a wry glance that spoke volumes concerning her amusement at the predicament she had found me in. Shame banished any thoughts of surrender from my mind, and when my enemy stood upright, he could clearly see that the worm had turned.

"It isn't like it might appear, my Lady," he said, fashioning a hangdog expression to cast at Mamie. "Just a little amorous play between old friends. We can draw up whatever agreement Paulette wishes, and I'll sign it in exchange for only the figure previously discussed."

He apparently hoped that we would be mollified enough to drop our guard by this conciliation, and make to flee while we were distracted. Mamie was having none of it, however. Card was quick, but she was faster still. Before he had taken three strides she was upon him, catching his neck in the crook of one pretty arm and marching him back to where I stood, wondering at her speed and ferocity.

"There's no good at all in this one, Paulette," she said. "I never knew a bad apple to come right. You want to do the honors, or would you rather leave it to me?"

Card twisted like a snake in her grip, desperate to be free, but she drove her knee into the back of his thigh. We all heard the driftwood crack of the big bone. My wrist was itching frightfully as it worked upon its knitting, benefitted no little by the "tea" that Mamie and I had earlier shared. I was thick with hatred, and that emotion surely dripped from my voice as I answered her.

"Just allow me a moment with him, Mamie," I said, my own teeth extending themselves, "and then you may do what you will."

In London, in the heyday of my naivety, I'd commissioned a facial tattoo that I thought attractive and thoroughly witchy. Unfortunately, I soon discovered that this alteration disappeared upon completion, leaving my face unmarked and only manifesting itself under the most unfortunate circumstances. In time I learned that it could be summoned, and I called it forth now to present the most demonic appearance possible.

Card certainly suspected my intent, and he bucked violently again in Mamie's grip, although without effect. It had been an irksome issue for me, ever since my turning, that he had drained me and yet a weaker blood than his had made me what I am. I knew too little about my nature to be confident that what I was about to do would in any way counter that imbalance, but at the very least, I could do to him what he had once done to me.

His right leg still flopped uselessly as he struggled, and Mamie, a manic grin now splitting her freckled face, bent his head more violently while sliding her forearm under his ear, to expose his throat to me.

"Can't for the life of me see why you'd want to make this one feel good," she said, her smile undisturbed by Card's struggles, "but you're the one with a grudge to settle, so you just do exactly as you like."

I was afraid that if I hesitated I would fail to act at all, and I greatly wished to avoid giving him even the brief pleasure that such an inability on my part might provide, so I flew at him like a snake; the blow of my face striking hard against his skin, the snapping bite, teeth driven in to pierce, and a quick shake of my head to tear and force the flow. I swallowed twice before I realized what I was taking in, before the strength of it tightened the skin on my forehead, before I knew that I would always want more.

For Card's part, I wonder if he had ever, save during his making, been fed upon. Regardless, the pleasure took him hard, even had him rocking his pelvis toward me despite the broken leg. I fed on, feeling like I was flying out of myself with each swallow. For the first time, I understood how a drug could capture a mortal, especially a benighted child like the poor Coco Mamie and I had supped upon, and lure them again and again away from the real, hard world. When I thought I might never be happy again without that stolen blood, I jerked my head away and gave Mamie a short, guilty nod.

It was all I could do to sit, sprawled in the wet, disturbed sand, and wonder at what I had taken in. From it, I knew—albeit briefly—the ferocity of Card's greed, and also absorbed a taste of his powers. The latter began to fade as soon as I felt it, and its passing was almost enough to break my heart. I could do nothing but crouch there, absorbed in wonder and loss, as Mamie completed our revenge.

She broke his neck then, a negligent effort, and then brought her knee up hard again, this time just under the broken neck, to make sure the separation of the spine was wide and permanent before kicking the body into the water. Even before it sank, I began to catch hints of disruption at the edges of my vision, as if my focus was drifting in and out.

"What the *Hell...*" whispered Mamie, looking around in confusion. I pulled my glasses away from my eyes.

We were quite surrounded by Souls.

CHAPTER 17

"They claim to be the spirits of the unquiet dead," I explained, tucking the earpiece of my glasses into my collar before dabbing nonchalantly at my mouth with a kerchief I kept tucked up a sleeve. I then made rushes at several to assure my friend they posed no threat. The Souls either retreated ethereally or disappeared altogether. "They call themselves Souls, and for some reason are dedicated to sabotaging Alice Paul's efforts."

In truth, I welcomed the appearance of the apparitions, as I took their sudden manifestation as proof that we had successfully disposed of Bryan Card and, with his influence over the suffragist ended, the Souls were returning into the breach. Mamie Clover, despite being among the bravest creatures I'd even encountered, liked them not at all.

"Don't want no truck with hauntin's," she said, eying the apparitions cautiously. "So I think I'll leave this little problem to you. If we're done with your Mr. Card, and I do believe we are, I'll thank you to see me back to your place, packed, and on a train out of here. The faster I wash this city out of my hair, the happier I'll be."

I agreed, and it was soon done, with many thanks and promises to aid her in turn should the opportunity ever present itself. I waited at the station until her carriage had pulled away. There were Souls present in the depot and even on the platform, but none made as if to enter the train, so I was assured that Mamie would have a peaceful, if boring, journey home.

My next chore was to visit the suffragists' offices. I was pleased to find the door to the inner sanctum open and Alice Paul seated at her desk, though I'd been forced to run a veritable gamut of Souls outside the building. The little brunette looked more wan and drawn than usual, but the fire in her strange violet eyes was by no means banked.

How she knew I did not understand, but clearly she was aware that I had negated Card's hold upon her. She indicated that I should enter and shut the door behind me, and rounded upon me as soon as it was closed.

"I suppose you've come expecting a thank you, Miss Monot? Well, you shall not get one from me. Without your involvement in our doings, that creature would never have interfered with me. And I'll have you know that, despite his powers, I would have thrown off his influence on my own with but a bit more time."

I could not suppress a smile at her ferocity, and quickly sought to calm her.

"Any actions I might have taken, Alice, were for my own purposes and not your aid. And I am wise enough to expect no gratitude from you. I would have had to settle matters with Bryan Card sooner or later; his interference into your doings only brought that situation to a head. More to the point, do you feel yourself again, ready to wrest control of the movement back from our poor, overworked Lucy Burns?"

The little woman rolled her eyes at the thought of her companion being overextended. Obviously, Alice still believed that Lucy's dedication to their shared cause was not as ardent as it ought to be. She glanced again at the door, as if to assure its closure, and then, fixing me with her eyes, spoke in a far less confrontational voice than she had earlier employed.

"What he did to me, Miss Monot, did you do the same to Lucy?"

It was clearly not a time for equivocation.

"I'm unaware of exactly what you and Bryan Card might have done, Alice, but I can assure you that during our time together, Lucy and I enjoyed lovemaking in every manner open to two women, but that is not what you're really asking, is it?"

She frowned, as if resisting the mental images my statement had called forth. "No. I mean, did you force yourself upon her...upon her *mind*?"

"I had no need nor wish to do so with her, and neither did Card," I said. "Lucy has quite a healthy interest in sex, and she was attracted to both of us naturally. Once she'd experienced the pleasures of the blood feed, her only concern was to repeat it as often as she could, regardless of the partner involved. You, on the other hand, are far less... *sensual*...than she, and I'm sure my enemy tried his charms upon you before he resorted to Entrancement and found them lacking. I'm certain I would encounter the same resistance, and without capturing your will would be quite unable to seduce you."

She stiffened.

"I don't believe you could do so, Miss Monot, even if you bent all your talents to it."

I had no wish to argue the point, though I was quietly confident that my powers of Entrancement, though less than Card's had been, would be quite capable of entrapping her, so I decided to turn the conversation in another direction.

"Be that as it may, Alice," I said, my eyes safe behind my lenses, "you may rest assured that whatever happened to you while under the influence of Bryan Card is in no way on your conscience. You can be confident that he is no more, and will never again twist your mind to his own desires. The challenges you face now are as they were before: Carrie Catt's hatred and the things that call themselves Souls. You were proof against them once, and I trust you will manage to be so again."

This information seemed to calm her, though I could still read the horror in her eyes. Alice Paul had a mind of strength and imagination far surpassing the norm, and to lose control of it must have been especially galling for such as her.

"Then, though I denied I would do so, I find that I must thank you, Miss Monot," she said. "And as for the future, since Mr. Wilson seems determined to keep our nation out of the great European battles, let's just see how he copes with a war at home."

CHAPTER 18

That foreign conflict had in fact grown increasingly complex, with a seemingly endless reconfiguration and reshuffling of alliances. An entire continent, it appeared, was facing its enemies across wandering miles of trenches. New horrors such as poison gas and an air war, with craft that appeared as delicate as butterflies but which proved as terrible as dragons, came into play. After a hiatus, Germany also returned to unrestricted submarine warfare, raising the ire of many in the United States.

If the election of 1916 was seen as a referendum, it made clear how conflicted the nation was about the "European struggle." Wilson, who had campaigned on the slogan "he kept us out of war," barely eked out an electoral victory over the more hawkish Hughes Though Wilson strove mightily to affect some sort of diplomatic solution, his efforts came to naught. The realization seemed to be creeping into the national consciousness that America would not be able to avoid taking part in the hostilities.

This suited my investment strategy, but I found the process excruciatingly slow and more than once had to make adjustments to my speculations to accommodate the glacial stirring of a hesitant nation. Indeed, Germany and her allies seemed to take heart in America's reluctance to enter the war, and she increased the depredations of her submarine fleet in hopes of starving England into submission. Thus, the allied blockade thwarted my ability to trade with Germany, while that nation did her best to frustrate my efforts to wring a profit from the English. It was a maddening time to dabble in finance, though I never ceased making money.

Lead by their reenergized general, the suffragists threw their voices into the mix with a campaign they dubbed "The Silent Sentinels." These women, mostly young, respectable, and often including both Alice Paul and Lucy Burns, positioned themselves at the very gates of the White House and armed themselves with banners comparing America's lack of suffrage to the worst of the human rights abuses in Europe. As their name implied, they neither chanted nor made speeches, letting their signage speak for them as they held a quiet witness to what they saw as Wilson's hypocrisy.

At first, they were well tolerated. Even the President seemed sympathetic to their cause. It is rumored that he had coats sent to the Sentinels in inclement weather and his kitchen even provided them with tea. America was so evenly divided on the matter of war that the demands of the suffragists were, if not universally agreed with, at least recognized as a legitimate viewpoint and not treated with outright hostility.

For reasons that were admittedly purely selfish and financially driven, I determined to upset this precarious national balance. There are Kin in all of the so-called civilized nations of Europe, and though we care little for the politics of the warm, we are often forced to react to them. I had maintained contact with those of my Kind who also dabbled in international trade, regardless of which side of the trenches their home nations found themselves upon.

In particular, during the early days of the allied blockade, I had through the good offices of Mamie Clover made contact with one Hilde Schurter, a Kin of Swiss nationality. By virtue of her country's neutrality she had helped me to continue trading with those nations whose markets had been blocked to me. That commerce had proved mutually profitable, and inclined *Madame la Suisse* to respond favorably when I next approached her.

We had need to be circumspect, given the nature of our discussions and the serious repercussions we could have faced. But my Kind are very accustomed to saying one thing and meaning another. I was able to convince Schurter that, should the U.S. enter the war and we both have advance knowledge of the fact, the potential for profit would be staggering. Still, we started cautiously.

Much of our correspondence was handwritten and cluttered with nonsensical references to the antics of children and pets to confound would-be censors. The dates of each letter, which we manipulated when necessary, provided clues to the cipher used in the next. On what were presented as special occasions (imaginary birthdays, anniversaries, condolences, and such) we would resort to telegrams. Over time, we were able to establish a tit-for-tat interchange in which I would provide profiles of "the mood of the man on the street," and thus America's feelings regarding the war. With this, Hilde was able to parlay with Kin in Germany for tidbits of information that might prove useful to me.

It was through this pedestrian exchange of data that I learned of a purported telegram being sent by German Secretary Arthur Zimmerman to his nation's Ambassador to Mexico, asking the latter to convince his host nation to join an alliance with Germany should the United States enter the struggle. This interested me intensely. Because of the destruction of telegraph cables by nations on both sides of the Great War, the message was forced to make its way through a relay station in Southern England. From there, its signal was to be boosted for the transatlantic crossing.

With this information in hand, I was able to inform another foreign contact dating from my time in England. This was one Margaret Dawes, who with calculation had formed a dalliance with a mortal man at the lower rungs of the British government, and immediately recognized the significance of the telegram's transmission. Thus, the letter was intercepted and translated.

Because of the intricate machinations of foreign policy, and the desire to protect English code-breaking capabilities from German discovery, it was some time still before the contents of the so-called "Zimmerman missive" were made public. It was longer still before anti-English forces in the U.S. were convinced of its authenticity. Eventually, the telegram's author verified its contents himself. Pushed to a point of no return, on April 2, Wilson asked Congress for a declaration of war to make the world safe for democracy."

It would seem that this stated mission played directly into the hands of the suffragist's "Silent Sentinels." Alice Paul saw it as such and was quick to draw attention to the jarring disconnect implied by the statement. Neither she nor I, however, had correctly anticipated how the public's perception of this criticism would change now that Wilson had become a "wartime President."

CHAPTER 19

I must also give credit where credit is due, and recognize the Souls for their role in fomenting the increased hostility encountered by the suffragists almost immediately upon the declaration of war. The influence asserted by those creatures benefitted greatly from having an edge to rub against and thus sharpen, and the media, always eager to engage in jingoism and ably assisted by the steady outpouring of propaganda as part of the "Creel Committee's" daily "Bulletins" (also called the Committee of Public Information, this was a government agency charged with soliciting public support for war), worked hard to paint America's new enemies in the darkest of colors. Suddenly, the Sentinels were seen to be providing aid to the foes of democracy, and the mood of the public turned ugly.

Wilson, who had worked so diligently to avoid American participation in the war, seemed to lose all tolerance for dissent now that a role in those hostilities had been forced upon him. Thus, he turned a blind eye as the public, unhindered by the Washington police, quickly escalated their abuse of the suffragists from the verbal to the physical.

That the Sentinels had vowed to maintain a silent protest served only to feed the fire of this anger. There is a class of men—and women, too, if I am to be completely truthful—who are inflamed by passivity. Thus, the more the suffragists bore their abuse in silence, struggling only to uphold their banners when the crowds made to rip these away, the more pointed the attacks upon them became. It was, the beleaguered President must have realized, a public relations nightmare in the offing.

Perhaps in an attempt to counter this, the police began to take on a more direct role in managing the militants; preempting, by their actions, those of the crowds. The right to public protest and assembly was still (at least officially) sacrosanct, and to violate that in a bald-faced manner would only reinforce the message the Sentinels were struggling to convey. To circumvent this, a series of contrived reasons for disrupting their activities were concocted, the most commonly used of which accused them of disrupting the movement of vehicles and persons in the area.

If anyone expected the women to fade quietly away in the face of these escalations, they had underestimated the opponent they faced in Alice Paul. As soon as one group of protesters was driven off and their signage destroyed, the little brunette deployed another with banners more incendiary than the first. With the Souls urging the public and the police to greater violence, and Alice apparently relishing the increased intensity of the struggle, the upshot was quite predictable. In July, the first group of Sentinels, Miss Paul included, were arrested on charges of obstructing traffic, convicted, and incarcerated at the notorious Occoquan Workhouse.

Originally established as an "industrial farm" for the rehabilitation of short-term prisoners (drunkards, vagrants, abusers, and prostitutes formed the core of its target clientele), the Workhouse, whose barracks had been built by its inmates from bricks they had formed themselves, was certainly unlike anything the suffragists, most of whom were women of some standing in society, had ever experienced. The public initially recognized this imbalance between crime and punishment, and the resulting outcry led to pardons for most of those first sent there. Before their release, however, did their fear, however well controlled, titillate the monster at the Workhouse's core? This is speculation, but I suspect that it did.

Alice Paul knew nothing of this, and was even unaware of the creature whose appetites might be so piqued by her efforts, or of how their histories would intertwine. Instead, she saw in that public outrage a tool that she could use, and once released, pushed for the protests to continue. I urged her toward restraint, as the manipulation of the Souls ever amplified the voices in opposition to her aims; but she was adamant. Though all of those arrested were offered the choice of a fine instead of imprisonment, and while most if not all of Paul's followers could easily have afforded the amounts demanded, the little brunette urged them one and all to choose the Workhouse over any payment that could be construed as an admission of guilt.

I was not entirely certain of the wisdom of this approach. Since the destruction of Bryan Card, the Souls had become quite common, and I was certain that the doors and bars of the Workhouse would offer no impediment. Those charged with administering that institution, hardened as they must already be from their dealings with society's castaways, would surely be susceptible to the whispering of the spirits of discord. Little did I suspect then what sort of creature lead that administration, and how the banquet of suffering he would soon enjoy would affect him

There was another matter related to the Souls that perplexed me as well. Though Carrie Chapman Catt was still affiliated with NAWSA and nominally in competition with Alice's National Women's Party, she had turned away from the state-by-state strategy she had once championed and thrown her support behind the push for a constitutional amendment guaranteeing women's suffrage.

Going so far as to characterize this effort as her own "Winning Plan" to earn the vote, Catt may still have been in competition with the younger suffragists for credit and attention, but it seemed she had lent her own hand to the plow that Alice Paul had been guiding. This being the case, why were the Souls more numerous and vociferous than ever?

CHAPTER 20

As the suffragists cycled into and out of prison, for the most part quickly pardoned despite Alice's escalations, I decided that I must again interview Mrs. Catt on hopes of obtaining new information on the manifestations that fancied themselves Souls. It was clear that those entities opposed my intended meeting, as they quickly set out to impose what obstacles they could.

They swarmed around me as I approached the hotel in which the NAWSA president held residence, and made every effort to influence the mortals in my vicinity to interfere with my progress. A glimpse of my unfiltered eyes soon dissuaded even the most adamant of these, and the Souls themselves maintained a wary distance.

When I arrived at the hotel, I stopped by the front desk to inquire as to Mrs. Catt's room (I had telephoned first requesting an interview, but had neglected to confirm this important information, since the suite in which she stayed was not the same she had occupied previously). There was still a blur of Souls infesting the lobby, so I wasn't surprised when the woman who staffed that desk attempted to confound me.

After first flipping through a ledger in an effort to appear helpful, she looked up at me with manufactured regret.

"I'm sorry," she said, "but we don't seem to have anyone by that name in residence. Are you certain you're at the correct establishment?"

Already a tad weary as a result of the interference I'd previously encountered, I was still loathe to waste the effort of my eyes on this petty functionary, so I replied with exaggerated politeness.

"No," I said, "I'm quite certain I have the right hotel. Furthermore, I spoke to Mrs. Catt not thirty minutes ago and she is expecting my visit. Perhaps you'd be so good as to have a second look? I've hurried because I know she dearly hates to be kept waiting."

Though I had not asked to speak to her superior, perhaps that threat was implied in my tone. To be more charitable, it could be that the receptionists' commitment to her duty was strong enough to overcome the influence of the Souls, now that they had fled the immediate area to avoid me. At any rate she consulted her paperwork again and, with a sweet apology, directed me to room 201.

I was grateful to learn that the woman was only on the second floor, as I had already decided to take the stairs rather than run the risk of further delay at the hands of the elevator operator. I found her door and, upon knocking, was once again in the company of Carrie Chapman Catt.

She recognized me immediately though I had made no reference to our prior conversation when on the telephone. She even recalled my name, giving evidence of a mind that was sharp as ever despite the political struggles she had endured, and the recent loss of her husband. Regardless of whether he occasionally turned an appreciative eye to younger women as Alice surmised, he had remained Carrie Catt's steadfast partner to the end.

"Miss Monot, isn't it?" she said, leading me into a comfortable sitting room where tea had again already been set out in anticipation of my coming. "To what do I owe the pleasure of a second visit?"

I accepted the offered cup and seated myself, taking a moment to study the other woman. Mrs. Catt remained an imposing female, but the passing time since our last meeting told clearly on her features, and I thought I glimpsed a carefully reined-in envy as she realized that I did not appear to have suffered the same deterioration, whether due to stress or time.

She was too polite, or perhaps too proud, to mention this discrepancy, and merely poured her own tea, and graciously awaited my reply.

"When we last spoke," I began, noting that none of the Souls seemed to have invaded her sanctum, "you mentioned that, while you held no truck with Spiritualism, it was once a commonly held belief among many in the suffragist community. You may think me gullible, but I have a great curiosity about such things, and wondered if you would elaborate for me."

Mrs. Catt sipped her beverage, apparently relieved that I had not come to talk about Alice Paul and the National Women's Party.

"Oh," she began, "such beliefs were rife within our movement a generation ago, and I fear they cost us much in credibility. But they were not the worst scandals with which we were saddled." She sipped again, as if wondering how deeply into the matter she should delve. "Surely you've heard of the scandalous Woodruff sisters, Victoria and Tennessee?"

I was not unaware of the names, and Catt had referred to Victoria during our former meeting. Though current events held little attraction for me while I was warm, I had worked in Manhattan, and despite the fact that it was well past their heyday, mention of the notorious sisters occasionally crept into conversation, often in the form of a ribald joke. So I nodded to indicate familiarity, and this seemed enough to encourage Mrs. Catt to continue.

"They were quite involved with Spiritualism, as I'm sure you've heard, and attracted sensation like a wet dog draws dirt." She paused, studying my reaction before continuing. "If that was the only brush they tarred us with, however, I would be grateful. But they also advocated free love, a perversely wide egalitarianism that sought to enfranchise even the benighted races, and other radicalisms that affiliated our movement with causes that were an anathema to right thinking men and women. It is likely that Tennessee, the younger of the two, actually engaged in prostitution!" She appeared to flush at the thought, and once more addressed her tea before continuing. "So you can see why I have been at great pains to separate NAWSA from the excesses of the past. The Woodhull sisters are, I believe, ensconced in England now, where whatever deviltry they get up to is far less likely to soil our efforts here."

"Surely," I said, choosing my words with care, "Victoria did not rise to power in the American suffragist movement without the backing of some of her sisters of the day?"

"Oh yes," the lady answered, "Mrs. Stanton remained a supporter long after Mrs. Anthony and the rest of the suffragists of the time turned away from Victoria's more radical ideas. And during the Woodhulls' time 'table rapping' and things of that sort were more or less a national craze, and many of the suffragists of the day were caught up in it. As I've said, though, we have since moved on and purged our ranks of such frivolity."

"What can you tell me about the nature of her beliefs?" I asked.

Mrs. Catt waved a hand impatiently, clearly weary of the topic.

"They were very much in line with the usual forms such folderol takes," she said. "Mrs. Woodhull claimed to have what I believe is called a 'spirit teacher,' some ancient Greek as I recall. Demosthenes? She maintained that he guided her on everything from speechifying to stock predictions. Though I've always thought that she owed Cornelius Vanderbilt, and Tennessee's womanly wiles, for the latter. I'm afraid I can't provide much more information than that. A pity that the sisters have made new lives for themselves in faraway England; I suspect you could learn more from the horse's mouth, as it were."

CHAPTER 21

I had little interest in crossing the Atlantic again, particularly now that the German submarines were making open warfare on American ships. Even the most seemingly harmless of these ships could be counted upon to be carrying materials to aid Britain. I was able to peruse those English newspapers available in the Capital, and through them learned something of the state of the Woodhull sisters in their adopted land.

Both women had married well, Tennessee becoming a Baroness, and their spouses had since perished. (There were unsubstantiated rumors that the younger Woodhull had a hand in her husband's demise). With the aid of their wedded partners (and their partners' fortunes) Victoria and Tennessee—now calling herself 'Tennie C'—had made great strides in recovering their reputations, and had modified their public opinions to suit. Both were said to be active in charitable work and had left their notorious pasts behind.

But had they, I wondered, left something else behind as well? The sisters themselves would prove to be difficult sources of information without direct contact and the urging of my eyes. They had gone to great lengths to distance themselves from the more colorful aspects of their American history (Victoria at one point having gone so far as to claim Alexander Hamilton as her ancestor), and any link to spiritualism would surely be among the footnotes they had sought to erase.

I believed that after thorough research I might discover a lever I could use to turn that rock over. Victoria's daughter from her first marriage (when she was but a girl of fifteen), lived with her in London. Zula Maude (formerly called Zulu) served as editor of her mother's journal, *The Humanitarian,* and had ambitions to become a playwright. Those who would live by the pen, particularly if they happen to be women, face extraordinary challenges and must always be alert for their main chance. If Zula Maude shared this eagerness with her sister scribblers, it might provide me with a path forward.

With that in mind, I arranged for the manager of one of my holdings to make a discrete inquiry. My representative wrote that the fund he controlled would be interested in financing the production of a new play in Washington D.C., and having heard of her ambitions, he believed that the Woodhull name might lead to some success. Would she be interested in pursuing such a project?

The reply, which came from the desk of Miss Zula Woodhull herself, arrived more rapidly than I'd dared hope, and exceeded my wishes in its eagerness as well. The lady waxed enthusiastic about the proposed project, and opined that her drama *Affinities* might be just the thing we were looking for. She included a *précis* of the plot, which I was pleased to see dealt with the subject of spiritualism, and enclosed several sheets from Volume 151 of the *Westminster Review* (1899) that, while it kept its powder dry concerning any predictions for what successes the drama might enjoy on stage, did refer to the author as "a lady of unquestionable talent" and described her plot as "original, striking, and thoroughly unconventional."

Even more pleasing was the news that Miss Woodhull would be visiting New York City in some weeks' time on other business (submarines be damned), and would be pleased to avail herself of a meeting in Washington during her sojourn. I instructed my operative to reply immediately, and to set up an interview between the author and myself. At the same time, he should arrange her lodging in a hotel that would impress upon her that she was dealing with people of some means.

The play itself did not interest me. It appeared to be a "modern" love story. The *Review* likened it to Ibsen in its use of its characters to interpret the author's views on society, and it employed the *Deus ex Machina* of "higher forms of common knowledge" inspired by electromagnetic research to bring its protagonists together. Regardless of my thoughts on its literary merits, I was determined to bring the thing to the boards in the belief that doing so would further my aims.

CHAPTER 22

Alice Paul, meanwhile, pursued her own goals with equal focus and energy. The mood of the public continued to harden toward the "Silent Sentinels." Though most were pardoned after serving little or no time in prison, she was determined to push the system to greater punishments in order to win headlines for suffrage. To that end, she brought herself to the front at every opportunity and was certain to be associated with the most inflammatory of their banners, including one which compared the president to the ruler of Germany, stating: "Kaiser Wilson, have you forgotten your sympathy with the poor Germans because they were not self-governed? 20,000,000 American women are not self-governed. Take the beam out of your own eye." It was not long before she received the reaction she sought.

On October 20, she was carrying a banner calculated to throw one of Wilson's own quotes in his face: "The time has come to conquer or submit, for us there can be but one choice. We have made it." She was arrested and sentenced to seven months in the Occoquan Workhouse. I'm sure the Souls at the scene indulged in a frenzy of celebration.

There was at that time still regular communication among the prisoners within and the suffragists without, and I was kept apprised of Alice's circumstances. There were enough of her sisters in the Workhouse with her that prison officials feared her exercising her leadership among the incarcerated, and accordingly placed the little brunette in solitary confinement for two weeks and restricted her to a diet of bread and water.

Though fierce in spirit, Alice Paul was physically a frail woman; some of that frailty could no doubt be attributed to the lingering effects of her prior imprisonment in England. This must have made her ordeal in the Workhouse at least familiar. At the end of her time in solitary she was considerably weakened, and reported that she was unable to walk unassisted. I was determined to aid her, but with Miss Woodhull's visit approaching I made the difficult decision to deal with that matter first and trust to Alice's ferocity to maintain her until I could offer assistance.

CHAPTER 23

I was aware that Zula Woodhull had experienced the highest of highs and the lowest of lows during her mother's tempestuous career in the United States, and that she now enjoyed a life of some privilege in England. So I had determined to arrange lodging for her that would eschew ostentation, yet assure her that she was in negotiations with people of some substance. Those criteria led me to book her into the established, but elegant, Hotel Harrington.

Success had inspired the edifice's owners, Harrington Mills and Charles W. McCutcheon, to expand the hotel, and work on this project was just beginning to get underway. Despite this, I was able to obtain a room with running water and a private bath that would be undisturbed by the accompanying bustle. I hoped that the evidence of enterprise would assure Miss Woodhull that, despite the strains of war, Washington was a vibrant and growing city.

My agent arranged for her travel from New York, and I allowed her an evening to refresh herself and recover from her journey before meeting her in the hotel's dramatic two-story marble lobby late in the afternoon upon the day following her arrival.

She was seated upon a plush couch when I entered, and I recognized her immediately from photographs and illustrations that I'd been able to obtain. Zula was no longer a girl, having already braved her fortieth birthday, but she remained a vital and attractive woman if not the great beauty that her mother was said to have been in her heyday. As she stood to meet me, I was immediately stricken by her composure and an air of quick intelligence that was to be expected of a woman who had grown up in the company of some of the most radical and innovative thinkers of the age.

"Mrs. Monot, is it?" she said, and I thought I detected a hint of an accent, no doubt acquired during her years in her new home. "I confess I thought I would be meeting someone male, and older."

"It's Miss, please," I replied. "And allow me to set your mind at ease. I enjoy full authority to discuss this matter with you, and to pledge the necessary funds should we come to an agreement. Your mother was, I think, but little beyond my age when she established the first all-female brokerage on Wall Street."

This seemed to satisfy her, and she resumed her seat while I took possession of an equally stuffed chair facing her.

"If it would not be an imposition," I continued before she could remove a sheaf of documents from her bag. "I'd much appreciate the opportunity to hear how your mother gets on before we begin. I confess I look upon her many accomplishments with something akin to awe."

I could see Zula slip behind a screen of caution as I said this, presumably fearing that my invitation had been only a ruse to dredge up information about the "Notorious Victoria" for a sporting paper or some other scandal sheet.

"As you certainly know," she began, "Mother lives a quiet life now, devoting herself to charitable causes and the single journal that I edit. She is far less, how shall I put this, newsworthy than she once was."

"Does she no longer consult the spirit world, then? I find it hard to believe that any woman, once granted that wisdom and comfort, would willingly give it up."

I knew I had gone too far before the words were quite out of my mouth. Miss Woodhull fastened her bag and made ready to stand.

"I have neither the inclination nor the authority to speak for my mother, Miss Monot. You invited me here, on what appears to be false pretenses, to discuss matters pertaining to my own career, which I am striving to forge independent of my illustrious ancestor. I will return to New York on the morrow. Thank you for the opportunity to experience this lovely hotel."

I did not rise, but pulled my cheque book from my purse and opened it on the low table between us.

"On the contrary, Miss Woodhull, I did not delude you in the least. In fact, I am prepared to fund the production of *Affinities* in a venue of your choosing, and to further provide you with an honorarium appropriate to the author of a work presented there. If, in return, you are unwilling to satisfy my curiosities, then perhaps I have misjudged my woman after all."

I could probably have entranced her then and there and obtained the information for nothing, but there were a number of Souls loitering about the lobby, their presence indicated as ever by a blurring at the edges of my lens-filtered sight. Since the ultimate goal of this exercise was to discover a weapon that could be turned against them, I had no wish to do anything that might hint at my objectives (and, in truth, the money was of little matter to me).

At any rate, she seated herself again, eyes on the open cheque book but not yet convinced.

"If I do answer your questions about my family," she said, "how am I to know that you will not seek to publish the revelations and Zula be damned?"

I had anticipated this objection, and brought forth another document from my bag.

"I have prepared a contract, which you are free to have examined by counsel if you choose. It outlines the offer I am prepared to make, and further pledges that any other matters discussed between us will be regarded as confidential and not to be released without your specific consent." I pushed this across the table toward her.

She took it up and perused it, no doubt with a caution born of the numerous injustices done to her family over the years. In fact, she did so twice, leaving me to sit and watch with no outward show of impatience. When this was done she regarded me again, with an air approaching shrewdness more than suspicion.

"It seems straightforward enough," she said. "I suppose there is little reason to incur the expense or delay required to bring attorneys into the matter. If you are prepared to sign this now in my presence, I will do the same, and you may ask away. I will only stipulate that our discussions steer clear of any exploration of the 'free love' question, or the Beecher case, as either of those carries the risk of sparking further litigation against my mother."

I readily agreed to this, believing that her discussion would wander where it would when underway, and with no intent to use any of the information gathered for purposes other than my own, which were quite specific.

Zula studied my face for a moment, as if there were proof of trustworthiness to be found there if only she looked long and well enough, and then flipped to the back page of the agreement and dated it, adding her signature with no little flourish.

Wordlessly, thinking silence befitted the formality of the occasion, I did the same, and passed the document back to her for safekeeping (having of course an unsigned duplicate for my records). I glanced around us. The shimmer of Souls was still present.

"Perhaps we could continue in your room, Miss Woodhull? I'm sure we would both be grateful for the increased privacy, and perhaps we could send down for a pot of tea to see us though our conversation?"

She agreed, and, followed by the insect-murmur of the Souls (whose caution in my presence would, I hope, prevent their accompanying us into such small quarters) we made our way to Zula's lodgings.

CHAPTER 24

When we arrived at her room, Miss Woodhull rang down for tea, first asking me if I required any additional refreshment. I declined the offer. As we had no wish to interrupt our discussion when room service arrived, we had no choice but to occupy the time while we waited.

I have little interest in (or talent for) small talk, but I assumed that Zula shared the peculiarity of those wed to the arts of being ready at the drop of a hat to discuss their "darlings" in detail. I was proved correct, for I asked her to provide me a summary of the plot of her opus and had no need to utter another word until the tea arrived. I was thankful for its delivery.

Once she had served and I had performed the mandatory ritual of bringing cup to lip, Miss Woodhull turned to the matter at hand.

"My mother does occasionally admit to spirit visitations still," she began, "but as to what she sees or doesn't see, certainly I cannot speculate. Her great guides of years past—

Demosthenes, Napoleon, Josephine—they are no longer with her. Mother claims that they have abandoned her."

"But you are not so certain?" I said, noting the hesitation in her voice.

Zula sighed, and refreshed herself with another sip before continuing.

"You are correct," she said. "Despite her protestations, I fear that my mother cast her spirit guides aside rather than they deserting her. Those great powers were, you see, important to the woman she was, and from whom she desperately seeks distance. Indeed, I myself have caught glimpses of them while in this country, and have never seen them in England."

I couldn't keep the surprise from my voice.

"You say that you can see them too? And that you've actually glimpsed Mrs. Woodhull's personal guides in America since your return?"

She appeared affronted by these questions, and her anger showed in the tone of her voice.

"You think me less than her, then? I assure you that I am every bit the spiritualist my mother is, and would have matched her on the world stage as well, had not my best years been consumed with caring for my damaged brother Byron."

I was quick to attempt mollification.

"I believe no such thing, Miss Woodhull. And I am hopeful that the forthcoming production of your drama will do much to establish your reputation as an independent intellect. But tell me, do you believe these entities seethe at their abandonment, and that their anger could manifest as ill will toward any others among the living?"

She would clearly have rather discussed her writing than the subject at hand, but acknowledging the agreement she had signed, Zula went on.

"I do sense resentment there," she said. "For though I have glimpsed Demosthenes and the others, they make no effort to communicate with me, and seem eager to distance themselves from my presence. You must remember, however, that these spirits had allied themselves with my mother, who, I presume, aided them in the difficult transition from their realm to our own. Surely even you, Miss Monot, were you transported to another life and there abandoned, would feel ill used as a result?"

This salvo struck too close to home, and I wondered for a moment if Zula knew more than she should, but I soon put the accuracy of her conjecture down to mere coincidence, and pressed forward.

"I take your point," I replied. "Now answer me this—and think well upon it before you do—is it possible that the spirit world, in its resentment, might turn its energies toward confounding those who now champion the cause most associated with that realm?"

She eyed me slyly, and even laughed a little, though the chuckle was bitter.

"So now we come to the crux of the matter, do we not, Miss Monot?" she said. "Could it be that you have fallen under the spell of Alice Paul, who seems willing to turn the world upon its head if doing so will allow her to accomplish what my mother could not?"

"The struggle for suffrage is a hobby to me, no more," I said, having no wish to give Zula what she might consider an edge. "You see, I've found that a woman with wealth enough feels little sting at her lack of the vote. But I have taken some small interest in the affairs of Miss Paul and her allies, and I have personally observed the efforts of what I presume may be spirits attempting to counter those aims."

Zula studied me again.

"So you are a spiritualist as well?" She seemed to find this difficult to fathom. "From your admitted affinity for the dollar I would think you more allied in sensitivity to my Aunt Tennie than my mother. Besides, I've always suspected that spiritual visitations were more a matter of convenience than belief for the former. Tell me, what exactly is it you hope to learn from me?"

Already in the water, I determined to wade still deeper.

"As I've said," I began, "there seem to be forces akin to your spirits seeking to counter the efforts of the suffragists today. Though I personally have no dog in that hunt, as they say, I think you'll agree with me that any women seeking social change face obstacles enough without having to joust with the supernatural. If I could, I would find a way to end this spiritual interference and allow history to proceed as it will, uncontaminated by such entities."

"I believe mother might manage to accomplish what you seek," Zula said, "but you are unlikely to lure her here despite your wealth, as she is well enough set up herself, and has no love lost for the nation that so railed against her. Beyond that, I am unaware of any path forward for you. I suppose, were you willing, we could attempt a séance, you and I, and see if under those constraints we might be able to force communication from the spirit guides."

I had anticipated this proposal, but that did little to ease my discomfort at the prospect. Despite the indisputable evidence of my own eyes, which told me that the Souls were both inhuman and present in some numbers, I couldn't shake my long-held convictions that séances were potentially dangerous. My trepidation was in no way alleviated when, upon my agreeing to this experiment, Zula informed me that it would have to take place on the morrow, and she required "time to prepare."

CHAPTER 25

I arrived at the appointed hour fully expecting some sort of choreographed extravaganza, complete with table-rapping, ectoplasmic materializations, and haunting voices from the void. I was surprised when Zula opened the door dressed much as she had been the day prior, in a modest but clearly expensive dress clasped tight at the collar with a brooch, and her ankles modestly hidden. There was nary a hint of incense in the air.

She took my wrap, noting with apparent satisfaction the water upon it, as it had just begun a light misting rain. The room appeared quite unchanged, and I scanned without success for any new addition that could conceal the sort of paraphernalia I'd anticipated.

Miss Woodhull watched my examination with wry interest.

"I hope you're not disappointed, Miss Monot," she said. "Clearly you expected more in the way of spectacle?"

I certainly felt "caught out" by her statement, but I tried to keep my reply less than revealing.

"In truth, I did not know what to expect, this being my first venture into these mysterious waters. Are you ready, then?"

"I am," Zula said. "You see, rather than the humbuggery you clearly anticipated, my preparations were largely internal. A matter of closing my mind to distractions, and opening it to those voices that might attempt to reach it. I had an early dinner, a refreshing sleep, and a day of meditation in anticipation of your visit. The rain, which some feel is conducive to spiritual action, is a bonus I had no control over. In short, I believe I am as ready as ever I shall be."

Her quarters, though among the best the Harrington had to offer, were not especially spacious. Zula had made do, arranging a couch and chair on either side of a long, dark, intricately designed coffee table. Upon this, she had placed three candles and a small piece of bread. Off to one side were a bell, a knife, and one of the hotel's salt cellars.

She explained that we were to sit opposite one another and clasp hands across the intervening tabletop. Before we began, she closed the curtains, muffling the ever-present city sounds already hushed by the rain to a soft buzz. It not being fully dark yet, there were no lamps to douse, though I don't know whether she would have deemed such action necessary if there were.

I asked if she had any specific instructions for me, a chant, perhaps, that I should intone to lure our spirits like a salt lick will draw a cow. Zula assured me that was not necessary, and that I had only to rein in my skepticism; remain seated; focus my thoughts upon Demosthenes, with whom we would attempt to speak; not break the contact of our hands regardless of what I might hear of see; and remain silent.

As we seated ourselves, my hostess explained the items on the table. The bread was an offering; the candles an invitation; and the bell, blade, and salt all forms of defense to be employed should the séance go awry. I thought I detected a bit of cynicism on Zula's part as she explained these matters, as though she secretly put little credence in them but was determined to honor at least the bare bones of tradition.

Controlling my doubts would, I thought, be the most difficult of the tasks she charged me with. As for the supernatural defenses described, I confess I found them quite laughable. I did not anticipate any sort of otherworldly occurrences, but should the Souls or anything of their ilk make an appearance, I hoped they would find Paulette Monot more formidable than any chime, condiment, or piece of kitchen cutlery. One would think that, given the shocks my preconceptions had received during my adventures in Africa and China, and my own dabbling in the supernatural, I would have known better.

CHAPTER 26

Miss Woodhull lit the candles from a single match, extinguished it, we joined hands, and we waited. She used no vocalizations (which rather disappointed me, having hoped at least for some sort of show), but sat with her head slightly bowed and her eyes closed.

And nothing at all happened.

I had neglected to wear my watch, thinking something so mechanical and prosaic might be unsuitable to bring to an attempt to reach across the spiritual planes. However, I had noticed a clock on the wall behind me before we took our positions, and as the minutes drained slowly away without interest or incident I occupied myself with trying to read its reflection in the centermost of the candlesticks.

While so occupied, I detected a flicker of movement in my peripheral vision. Raising my eyes, still safe behind their tinted lenses, I noticed that the flames above all three candles had begun to reach slightly in my direction, as if at the whim of some errant breeze. A quick inspection of the room behind them revealed no potential source of this disturbance, and then I noticed that Zula's grip on my hands had taken on new intensity.

I did not need that pressure to tell me that we were in the presence of something *other*; not with the blurring at the corners of my eyes, nor with the candle flames reaching further toward me; they were as long as fingers now, stretched far beyond the point at which any normal wind would have extinguished them. Zula glanced at the three protections on the table, but I quickly shook my head in the negative. I was not yet ready to sunder whatever connection had been made.

For that same reason, I dared not break our hand clasps to remove my glasses. Instead, I whipped my face up and down violently. This did not quite free me from the spectacles, their gold earpieces still clinging, but served to move them far enough down the slope of my nose to allow me to peer over the rims.

The candle flames flinched away, as if driven off by my glance, and returned to a weak tremble at the tips of their wicks. And there were Souls. They crowded the walls of the room, different faces appearing and disappearing as they struggled for vantage, their nattering devoid of clear speech but busy as a tree full of chickadees. As numerous as they were, however, they seemed unwilling or unable to venture further into the room. A glance at my hostess soon showed me the reason.

Her eyes were turned to the side, and following them, I soon beheld a wonder. As a trick picture will, with the merest shifting of the eyes, magically morph into something previously unseen, what had appeared to be merely empty space in front of Zula gradually gave birth to the strangest of apparitions.

It was a uniform, chalky white in color, without the slightest shade or tint in flesh or fabric. The man—for the entity presented itself as such—was clothed in a simple toga knotted over the left shoulder, leaving the right side of his muscled chest bare. His hair and beard, as uniformly pale as his skin and wrapping, were short and curled. I was well enough read to recognize that the vision before me was meant to represent Demosthenes, perhaps the greatest of the orators of ancient Greece and the being Victoria Woodhull had claimed as her spirit guide.

It was clear that whatever faith Zula had put in the séance, this was more than she had expected. Indeed, the woman was visibly trembling, and I believe that had my hands not clasped hers she might have grabbed for the salt cellar to fling it into the guttering flames. But hold her I did, more determined than ever to see this to its end.

The entity, fully materialized but still monochromatic (I thought it resembled a marble statue, though it seemed as limber as a man), was entirely focused upon Zula. This was perhaps because she had done the actual summoning. For her part, the woman was clearly terrified, and drew as far back from its looming approach as our joined hands would permit.

The thing spoke then. As with the Souls before, I cannot say with any certainty whether I heard an actual voice or if the words resounded directly in my mind. It was clear from the tone that the speaker was displeased, however, and as evident from Zula's face, which blanched to a shade as pale as that confronting her, that she heard the proclamations as well.

"I charge you with two wrongdoings," the thing that appeared as Demosthenes thundered, stabbing a cruel finger toward Miss Woodhull. "First, you are here as a false ambassador, appearing where I might have expected your mother. Worse still, you pollute this encounter with the death-that-walks, a thing that has neither the light of the living or the lightness of being of one who has fully passed on."

The latter accusation was clearly indicated for me, and since it was apparent that Zula was too overcome to offer any defense, I (not at all pleased with this condemnation) determined to speak for myself.

"You may be what you appear to be, and then again you may not, but I would caution you against making an unnecessary enemy of me in any case," I said.

The chitterlings of the gathered Souls rose in frequency at this apparent outrage, and the Greek whipped his head in my direction in a manner quite threatening.

"Silence!" it bellowed, and the candle flames started up again, streaming from their perches toward me despite my unshielded eyes.

Perhaps I should have been frightened, but in the years I've walked the world I have found fear to be a useful emotion only when it guides one to an appropriate strategy, and I saw no profit in showing retreat.

"If you seek to overmatch me with mere volume and parlor tricks, creature," I said, feeling my teeth begin to slip free all involuntarily, "you will learn that such will serve you poorly in a contest with Paulette Monot."

The assembled Souls seemed to go quite mad at my outburst, and breaking free of whatever had held them at a distance, charged at me as one. The thing that aped Demosthenes did the same, its spectral hands leaping toward my throat. I'm afraid that I reacted in kind, breaking my clasp with Zula in order to lunge at my attackers in turn. This gave Miss Woodhull (too preoccupied to notice the ill-considered emergence of my teeth) the freedom required to cast the contents of the salt cellar into the still burgeoning candle flames.

The room went quite dark, despite the fact that it was barely twilight, and a general smell of corruption swelled forth as if from an icebox left too long unattended. When the light returned I was standing with no sign of spirit or Soul around me, and Zula lay quite unconscious on the floor.

CHAPTER 27

My first thought was for my hostess' recovery, which was soon accomplished with the aid of a damp cloth and a small bottle of brandy discovered on a sideboard. When she was sufficiently restored to resume her seat, head in hands, I took a moment to thoroughly examine the room to disabuse myself of any lingering suspicion of hokum. The door remained locked as I had left it, and the windows were all shut and latched from within (we were high enough to make any access from those portals unlikely in any case). In short, whatever I had witnessed was not the result of the practiced trickery of the spiritual fraud.

By the time I'd completed my investigation, Miss Woodhull was more nearly herself. When I held the brandy to her lips and she took an impressive swallow, enough to make her cough, I assumed she was fit to be questioned.

"When you're quite ready, dear, and in your own words, would you tell me what just happened?" I was rather proud that I was able to keep my voice calm despite the lingering tension that still seemed to stiffen my body.

"It was Demosthenes," she said, liberating the glass from my hands to take another swallow. "Just as I've seen him before. But those other things, I have no idea what they were. I've never heard mother speak of the like."

"They are the inspiration for my curiosity, Miss Woodhull," I said. "They seem to be quite ubiquitous, and determined to upset the suffragists' plans. More to the point, why did the spirit attempt to assault me, and was I in any real danger?"

"He claimed you were a 'pollution,'" she answered. "But I cannot fathom why. It is as if he were not predicting your demise, but claiming you had already faced it. And yet you are as solid as I!"

This was not a conversational path I was eager to stroll, but there was information I needed still.

"I am certainly that," I said, patting her on the arm as reinforcement. "And yet he seemed about to strike at me. I had assumed such beings were insubstantial and thus unable to cause physical harm. Is that not so?"

"I believe that is the case," Zula said, but with more hesitation than I liked. "Though there are certainly tales of spiritual possession, the only accounts I have heard firsthand involve the temporary use of a medium through whom to speak. As you may know, Mother is said to have dictated her most rousing orations in such a state. But other than the experience leaving her drained, I have never heard her say she suffered as a result."

I wondered whether my particular circumstances might make me more susceptible to possession than the warm, but I had detected no exceptional power in the entity that tried to attack me, only a mindless fury. For her part, Miss Woodhull had clearly suffered at the very least a serious shock, but I could see no alternative than to move forward.

"We must try again," I said as gently as possible.

She was hesitant, but so potent is the allure of publication to the scribbling classes that I was confident that she would ultimately relent, and so she did, but with one significant caveat.

"Perhaps if I donned something of Mother's," she explained, "I might be able to assert additional control. Otherwise I fear we will merely repeat our former experience, and I have no wish to endure that again."

I acquiesced, and Zula set to rummaging through her luggage. I thought her baggage excessive for a visit of a few days, but I was neither ungrateful for this excess nor surprised, having some history with the theatrical clan. From the bottom of the second chest, she withdrew a hat box and from it, an ornate headpiece beribboned in black silk, which she affixed canted over her forehead with a pair of hatpins.

"This was one of her favorites, back in the day," Zula said, peering into a mirror as she adjusted the angle. It looked to me rather as if an overlarge crow had perched atop her skull, but I am myself not innocent of the occasional sin of fashion, and held my tongue.

When she was confident of the set of this remarkable headpiece, even checking it against an image of her mother in a small brooch she wore, Miss Woodhull announced herself ready to enter the breech once more, and we returned to the table. The salt cellar was replenished, the scattered grains swept away, and when all was in readiness, the candles reignited.

I removed my glasses prior to this event, the better to observe the details of the manifestation should it repeat itself. As before, we joined hands and Zula bowed her head in silent contemplation. Perhaps because of the previous success, we were not so long in waiting for an occurrence.

This time it was Demosthenes alone who put in an appearance, again manifesting in the peculiar trick-of-the-light manner which he had employed before. I immediately saw that my companion had been prescient in surmising that an article of Victoria's clothing might more effectively bind him, for though the spirit seemed to strain against those bonds, and glared at me with clear antipathy, he made no move to attack.

"She is still here!" he said, pointing an ethereal finger at me. "You are unaware of your own danger, Miss Woodhull. I charge you to break all contact with this abomination, or risk your own immortal soul."

I sensed that Zula, emboldened by the success of her ploy, was about to ask for clarification, and fearing where such a conversation might lead decided again to interrupt and question the apparition myself.

"I mean her no harm, spirit," I said. "Nor you, if you can refrain from attacking me. I seek only answers, but perhaps I am mistaken in thinking you able to provide them?"

He moaned. It was quite a satisfactory moan, very Shakespearian. I'm certain its intent was to cow me, but I had not come this far to be intimidated by theater. When the spirit was apparently finished with the fulsome display I calmly continued.

"Yes, yes," I said with an air of weariness. "You've made it quite clear that my presence offends you. You may take some comfort in knowing that I find your company unpleasant as well. If you will just tell me what I wish to know we can both be free of this disagreeable propinquity."

The thing that aped Demosthenes (for I was still uncertain that it had any true connection to the long-dead Greek) spoke not a word to this, so I took its silence for acquiescence and went on.

"There are three things I would learn from you," I began. "What are the entities that call themselves 'Souls;' from whence comes their antipathy to Alice Paul's suffragists; and how may I banish them?"

He stared at me in stony silence. I glanced at Zula, who was still noticeably pale and trembling. In fact she trembled so much that the black ribbons bedecking her unfortunate hat wriggled like eels. It was clear that I had reached an impasse and bold action was called for, so I determined upon a plan.

CHAPTER 28

Deciding that fortune never favors the timid, I tugged my hands free of Zula's grip, eliciting a start from her. The apparition faded briefly, as if to flee into insubstantiality, but gradually reappeared, its surprised eyes focused on the unlikely headpiece.

Taking this as evidence that my hunch had been correct, I rushed forward with my plan. Seizing the hat from Miss Woodhull's head with both hands and sending its pins flying, I jammed it down on mine and leered at the clearly horrified spirit from beneath its substantial brim.

"You will answer me now, I think?" I said.

Demosthenes began to moan again, but his ethereal heart was not in it, and he ceased when I snapped my fingers with impatience.

"So first," I demanded, "what are the things that call themselves 'Souls'?"

He appeared to struggle, as if cinched up in fearsome bonds. However, the effort was obviously futile, and after a brief display the spirit hung its head and replied.

"They are mine," he said. "I have called them into form from the energy available to me, in an effort to ease my loneliness since my abandonment by this woman's mother and aunt!" This was accompanied by the thrust of a ghostly finger at the clearly horrified Zula. I was not finished with my interrogation, however.

"So now we make a start at it," I said. "And why do they seek to thwart the efforts of the suffragists? Is this some pitiful revenge you seek upon those who deserted you?"

The spirit writhed again, fierce in his struggles, but I merely tugged the hat down more firmly atop my head and demanded. "Answer me!"

"No," he wailed. "No, I bear them no antipathy. It is the emotions their cause excites, the fierce and widespread antagonism. Such virulent fear and hatred was close to taking form even before my intercession. It was the easiest matter for me to work with."

Though I do not breathe per se, I felt as if I had run a race and was positively panting out of pure muscle memory.

"And now," I said, hands firmly upon the hat, "and now you will tell me how to dispel them."

The entity screamed as if pierced by a blade. Oh, how it struggled against my demand! It seemed about to break free of what held it, and loomed toward me in a manner most threatening. I was without fear at this point, but unfortunately, poor Zula was not. Her hands free since I had released them to snatch her hat, she grabbed at the bell and rang it, rang it, rang it.

Each chime was like a hammer blow upon the substance of Demosthenes, breaking him apart until there was nothing left but his relieved and lingering laughter.

When it was done, the candles had gone out, and the burnt-wax stink of their wicks lingered in the air. I turned to my companion only to see her draw back in terror, for it seemed the expression on my face must have been quite ferocious. I mastered myself (though not, I confess, without difficulty) and spoke in what I hoped were soothing tones.

"Rest easy, Miss Woodhull," I said. "Though I would have wished to converse further, I think I know what I must do."

Her fear dissipated as completely as the spirit guide, and she dared remonstrate with me.

"But Miss Monot," she said, "I fear I have undone all. After twice being banished Demosthenes will be proof against a third summoning. My timidity may have doomed your enterprise. Will you still keep up your end of the bargain?"

I had to smile at this. Despite the horrors the woman had witnessed, the production of her play was still uppermost in her mind.

"I will," I said, forcing a pleasant tone. The experience had not left me unaffected, and my bravery in the face of the spirit had been at least in part sham. "The entity may not have told us all, but it certainly revealed more than it wished to. I believe I can finish the puzzle from the pieces it so reluctantly provided. You shall have the funding for your production, and I charge you to move forward with it quickly. I believe that your *Affinities* may be exactly what this city needs."

She all but clapped her hands with delight. I wrote a first cheque then and there, enough to enable her to hire a hall and begin preparations, and gave her the name of an associate of mine whom she could tap for further funding or information as it became necessary. By the time I left she was clearly lost in the details of costuming and casting, as if we had not just wrestled with a supernatural terror. I mused on the strange nature of the arts and artists as I walked out into the early evening, pausing in the doorway to settle Victoria Woodhull's hat in a more fetching manner upon my head, and realizing that her daughter had failed to notice this obvious purloining

CHAPTER 29

As I made my way to the suffragist's headquarters, where a regular crew was now in residence to capitalize upon their leaders' most recent incarceration. I now and again removed my glasses and scanned my surroundings in search of Souls. I spied a few, though they seemed to maintain a greater distance from me than formerly. I wondered whether whatever force Demosthenes had used to congeal them into being was weakened. Then I realized that their apparent timidity could also simply be a result of my conflict with, and at least partial dominance of, their maker. Or perhaps it was due to the hat.

When I arrived at the office I found it all a-bustle, the determined women there busily distributing news of the ongoing arrests and rumored mistreatment of their comrades to whatever media outlets might prove sympathetic. I had to buttonhole several of them, and even remind them of my ongoing financial support for their cause, before I could learn the status of Alice Paul and Lucy Burns.

As I'd suspected, the two women were both now residents of the Occoquan Workhouse. This cruel incarceration—which Miss Paul had courted—provided the fodder for the bulletins and press releases the women on the outside were busily cranking out. Alice seemed willing to goad her keepers into using ever stronger measures to reap the publicity those punishments would generate. It was a strategy she had learned at the knee of Emmeline Pankhurst in England, which had nearly broken her constitution while there. I, however, found myself unwilling to allow her to become a martyr to her cause, however much she might have wished it, and determined to take action.

I learned from the suffragists in the office that messages were still getting into and out of the Workhouse, hence the ongoing news of Alice's travails, but that no words had travelled to or from Miss Paul herself since her confinement. I could have gained entrance to the facility through Enchantment, but once therein would be faced with too many guards to influence, (my ability is like to rifle and not a shotgun). It seemed the surest course of action would be to seek arrest myself, and to see how the cards lay when I was actually within the prison.

The suffragists had no shortage of volunteers willing to serve as Sentinels, and even had a schedule indicating when those who had been arrested and pardoned would cycle back into the fray. Through entreaty, logic, and the careful use of Enchantment, I was able to move my name to the top of their roster, to the relief, disappointment, or both, of the woman I displaced.

Knowing that the war had proved to be an inflammatory issue, both with President Wilson and the public crowds that often assembled to curse and harass the Sentinels (no doubt with invisible encouragement from the Souls), I asked the suffragists to craft a one-person sign for me, hung from a crossbar on a simple upright stake, to read, "Kaiser Wilson, Where Is Alice Paul?" I was confident this would prove aggressive enough to guarantee my arrest.

I was not mistaken. Not long after I had taken up position adjacent to the White House gates—dressed smartly and conservatively in black to compliment the hat that I still wore —a crowd gathered. Though the Souls were still hesitant to approach me, they had clearly determined that their stalking horses would have no qualms doing so. The men—and sadly, a few women—were rude and insulting in the extreme, and my lack of response seemed to infuriate them further.

The most common ploy seemed to be to insinuate that my placard was evidence of an unnatural affection for Alice Paul. Strangely enough, this seemed to my tormentors to be the vilest of accusations to throw at me. As I maintained my vigil, paying no mind to harangues, they grew louder and closed in around me.

It was inevitable that one of them would seek to destroy my sign, and I struggled in fitting silence against several adversaries who sought to do so. They were many, though, and seemed to draw inspiration from the bullies who took action first. In short order, I heard the *snap* of the splintering upright and found myself knocked to the ground; only to look up at one of my adversaries, clearly almost mad with fury and brandishing the broken-sharp base of my banner's stake at me in a manner most threatening.

It occurred to me that I might have inadvertently put myself in real danger. In dishabille from my fall, my skirts wet and dirtied and my headpiece lost, I crawled backward to put some distance between myself and my attacker. All around us, now a tableau of two, the angry crowd seemed to grow hushed as if eager for the denouement.

I could have fought or fled, at the risk of revealing something of my nature and thus complicating the situation beyond reprieve. Indeed, I readied to do so should the fatal thrust be attempted, but as my adversary paused, to gather either his courage or his will, he was struck down with a billy club and rough men in blue jerked me to my feet and into a waiting paddy wagon.

My dreams, it seemed, had come true.

CHAPTER 30

The police were none too friendly. My altercation had been dramatic enough to take precedence over the other suffragists' infractions. I found myself alone in the back of the vehicle, but for a taciturn patrolman for company. This individual spoke only to regale me with tales of the sort of treatment I could expect in the Workhouse, where, I was assured, I would "learn a lesson or two." He did not deign to reply to my questions about Alice Paul. He was also silent concerning the whereabouts of my hat, which I worried had either been picked up as a souvenir by my attackers or confiscated as evidence. If the latter, I was baffled as to what crimes it was supposed to imply.

Aside from my companion's savoring the horrors that awaited me, and steadfastly refusing to answer any of my questions, the ride to the Workhouse was uneventful. Once there, I was given the option to pay a fine, which amounted to some ten dollars, or be imprisoned. The amount was a trifle to me, but I chose the latter. None seemed surprised at my decision, as this had been the course of action selected by numerous suffragists before me. I was then sentenced to imprisonment for three days and moved into the general population.

I was also given a uniform: a drab, sack-like thing of rough cloth and a pair of horrid heavy shoes, and instructed to remove my own clothing and don the prison garb. I wondered whether I would be forced to disrobe in public, but the Workhouse had not yet descended to this level of barbarism and I was shown into a small room (none too clean) and there exchanged my stylish black dress for prison mufti. My own clothes were then taken away, although I was promised they would be returned to me upon release.

Suitably attired, I was informed that I would be put to work, the theory behind the establishment being that prisoners would pay their own way through some occupation there, and that the discipline of that labor would encourage good mental habits and teach skills that would be useful out in the world. Of course, these strictures were meant to be applied to the Workhouse's more traditional inhabitants: drunkards, addicts, prostitutes, and other members of the *demi monde*, so were not likely to contribute to the rehabilitation of the suffragists, who were by and large accomplished women from a higher level of society.

My assignment took me to a large room stocked with sewing machines. At each, a woman labored producing (irony of ironies) the selfsame crude uniforms with which we were all burdened. Guards patrolled the area, though lackadaisically, and were charged with stifling any communication that could lead to concerted action. These men were less than attentive, and through whispers and note-passing the inmates proved able to share such information as they found necessary.

Thus, I was able to learn where Miss Paul was kept. Actually reaching her, or indeed getting word to her of my incarceration, proved to be a far thornier problem. The situation was made worse by a steadily increasing presence of Souls in the prison, which soon manifested in growing truculence among the guards. The very atmosphere seemed to hint at a storm to come, adding a sense of urgency to my plans, ill-formed though they were.

The Workhouse was lit within, since the few, small windows had long since gone opaque with grime. I did not find it overly difficult to mimic the sleep patterns of my fellow inmates. We bunked all together in rooms corduroyed by rows of cots, so I was sure that with only a modicum of caution and a judicious use of Enchantment, I would be able to see to my own nutrition. In fact, I probably found it easier to do so than my fellow inmates; as the food was often worm-infested and worse, and made my own pretense of eating more the norm than the exception.

This soon worked to my advantage, as my three-day sentence had almost passed without my being able to contact Alice Paul. When I neared the end of that term, I was served a bowl of gruel. A glance at the surface of the sludge clearly showed stirring from the movement of something within, and with feigned outrage I flung the container to the floor. (To be honest, I would have eaten whatever life was in it if driven by need, and had done as bad before)

Several other inmates immediately mimicked my protest, and as the apparent ringleader of this little insurrection, my sentence was extended to two weeks. That evening, whilst lying in my cot attempting sleep (for while I could rest during what was evening beyond the walls, I still found this difficult) I rolled over to see the inmate closest to me wide awake, and her open eyes fixed upon me.

I did not know the girl, but her brightness of eye and clear intelligence marked her as a likely suffragist rather than one of the more traditional inhabitants, and she had obviously witnessed my rebellious actions earlier in the day. She whispered to me—and in that place whispering was, by necessity, so soft that it almost required a facility for reading lips.

"That was a brave thing you did," she mouthed, "but be wary of such actions or you may end up locked alone, and suffering the same outrages that I fear are even now being inflicted upon poor Alice Paul."

This statement earned my attention, and through a further hushed conversation—interrupted when one of the guards passed by, as they did at regular intervals—I was able to gather additional information about where the little brunette was held. The location was at best uncertain, for I had no map of the establishment and it was quite warren-like in its layout, but I determined to act on this data when the first opportunity presented itself.

CHAPTER 31

The structures in the Workhouse were built of brick which the inmates mixed, shaped, and fired themselves. The prison was not monolithic, but instead consisted of a number of separate buildings clustered in a Reformatory Division, and a walled and distinct Penitentiary sector. Most of the suffragists—myself included—were housed in the former. We were, after all, accused of such relatively minor crimes as disrupting traffic, there being no law restricting freedom to assemble. The more secure cells, on the other hand, were situated in the latter, and were small, dank, dark, and fearsomely barred. Thus, an inmate could not simply stroll from one area to the other without being challenged on numerous occasions.

In truth, I had no specific plan, just an urge to see for myself that Miss Paul was well and to offer her whatever sort of support she wished. It could be, too, that I felt guilt—an emotion I seldom indulge in—over dallying with Zula Woodhull while the suffragists escalated their protests. There had been no immediate benefits from that experiment despite my conviction that I had come away from it with important information. The Souls were ever more present, and seemed to have the ear, as it were, of every guard I spied.

So it was with no clear strategy that, once my roommates gave in to exhausted slumber, I crept from my cot to explore. The door to our building was monitored of course, but I was ready, with my glasses in my hand, as I approached the individual charged with securing it.

He had clearly felt the influence of the Souls, and was in no mood for nonsense.

"'Ere you," he said, already raising his club, "git back to yer bed or ye'll wish ye had!"

The urgings of the Souls, who were even then encouraging him to violence from a distance, were no match for my naked eyes. Before he could strike, I had captured his will, and moments later was beyond the building in the yard, with a general idea of the direction of the Penitentiary Division where I assumed Alice Paul was held. The guard, with no memory of our interaction despite the chittering of the Souls (which, I was confirming, could only cajole and not inform), resumed his position and continued vigilance over the building I had left.

Since the grounds were empty of inmates at night, I simply exercised the ability to avoid attention that comes natural to my Kind to make my way around and between the brick structures. These were numerous enough to present a kind of maze, but I made my way in the direction of the more secure area of the Workhouse.

When I finally came within sight of that compound, however, I realized that I had underestimated the difficulty of my undertaking. Where the Reformatory area was surrounded by wire fencing—hardly a challenge for such as I —the Penitentiary was a formidably walled enclosure. There was only one visible gate where an access road entered, and no less than a half dozen guards milling about.

I was squatting in the dark to consider my options when I suddenly found myself illuminated by the light of a dry cell torch. A guard, possibly en route to relieve one of the groups ahead of me, had come up from behind while my attention was occupied. He blew his whistle straightaway, which resulted in the group at the walled gate rushing toward the light and hence toward me.

Silently cursing my own lack of caution, I had but moments to determine a plan of action. It seemed neither fight nor flight would serve under the circumstances, since both would result in a general alarm. The latter, if successful, would engender a fear on the part of the staff that could only bode ill for the suffragists still imprisoned. Thus, I decided to surrender peacefully and to plead confusion.

Despite the latter, and my own conviction that the poor food and foul conditions in the Workhouse could easily be believed to leave a proper young lady disoriented, I found myself hard used. I was struck repeatedly with blows that would have sorely injured a mortal woman, then flung back into the building I had escaped. I fell to the floor there, feigning the sort of damage that would been expected. The guard I had entranced was understandably confused by my appearance. I feared he would suffer a severe disciplining, the reason for which he would never comprehend.

Many eyes followed me as I slowly made my way back to my cot, the disturbance having awakened all but the most exhausted of my roommates. Even those last few were soon roused as the lights were brought up and a thorough bed check was conducted. When we were once again in darkness, I could hear the soft susurration of whispers as information was passed from one inmate to another. Behind it all was the gleeful chattering of the Souls. I lay abed, chastising myself for my arrogance and clumsiness. The only solace I could take was that my quick surrender had spared my fellow inmates from more brutal treatment than they were already subjected to.

I allowed this thought to lull me into an uneasy slumber, despite the fact that the night was still upon us. Events that were soon to come would negate any satisfaction I might have taken from my caution. It is difficult to imagine that the repercussions that resulted from efforts to protect myself could have exceeded the violence with which the Workhouse was soon to erupt.

CHAPTER 32

Nothing happened immediately, although the signs of the impending terror were everywhere to be seen if one opened one's eyes to them (I fear I did not). The Souls were more prevalent than ever. They still avoided my approach; but they were always around me, as a cloud of gnats will hover just inches from a face liberally doused with pyrethrum oil. After my signature failure reaching Miss Paul, I resolved to make no further efforts until I had a better understanding of the situation. To that end, I occupied my time collecting what gossip was available and doing what I could to ease the plights of those suffragists in my immediate company.

Despite the various efforts of the authorities to limit communication, I was able to regularly access information on the little brunette's condition, though such reports were fragmentary and often contradictory. As I've mentioned before, she was kept on hard rations in lonely confinement, and there is little doubt that these weakened her already challenged constitution.

I first heard reports that she had died. I confess was on the verge of committing a dramatic act of violence—and the devil take the consequences—when a second, seemingly more accurate report surfaced that she had grown frail to the point of being unable to walk and been transferred to the prison infirmary. There, despite her poor condition (and providing clear evidence of her fierce, even foolish, courage) she was said to have embarked upon a hunger strike, a course of action that was rapidly imitated by many of my cohorts. I pretended to join her as if in sympathetic alliance, although this merely made it easier to explain my lack of interest in the food

Reports were regularly smuggled in to me from my financial representatives beyond the walls, as I had insisted that I be kept appraised of Zula Woodhull's progress in staging her drama. I learned she was already well into rehearsals, and seemed to have taken my request that she proceed with all due urgency to heart (or perhaps she merely feared I could cut off my funding at any moment, and only hurried to being her piece to the stage before I might do so).

The voluntary starvation embarked upon by many of the prisoners soon began to have repercussions that the authorities could not ignore. More than one woman fell into a faint across her sewing machine due to hunger, and as increasing numbers of them became bedridden and productivity dropped, the mood of the guards (goaded, as always, by the ubiquitous Souls) continued to worsen.

Meanwhile, Alice has been moved to a psychiatric ward and was being threatened with internment in St. Elizabeth's Asylum if she did not break her fast. She stood firm, however, and the prison staff, fearful that she might indeed die and, perhaps taking a page from the book of horrors the suffragist had endured while learning from the Pankhursts in London, began force-feeding her three times a day, violently inserting a tube deep into her throat and pouring through it a high-protein mixture of raw eggs and milk. I later learned that one of the attending physicians remonstrated with his colleagues at this, stating that she had "a spirit like Joan of Arc, and it is useless to try to change it. She will die but she will never give up."

This fell on deaf ears, and taking her stubbornness as a clear sign of madness, the staff attempted to have her judged insane so the threatened transfer could be accomplished. They failed at this, however. The psychiatrists called upon to make the determination proved as unwilling as the ward physician had been to do their masters' bidding. One of them, in defying the rush to declare her mad, stated bluntly that "'courage in women is often mistaken for insanity."

In response, and in another futile effort to break her will, the administrators demanded that she be denied sleep, ordering a bright electric lamp be shined on her face at regular intervals whenever she seemed about to doze off. Though this no doubt further weakened Miss Paul, it did nothing to lessen her resolve.

I learned much of this later, but the reports that did leak out quickly made their way beyond the walls of the Workhouse, where an ever busy staff of suffragists made sure that every injustice was reported to the media. These revelations served to embarrass the Wilson administration, which in turn increased pressure upon the prison administration to bring the protesters in line.

Such demands fell most heavily on the shoulders of one W. B. Butler, superintendent of the Occoquan Workhouse and an individual I was to come to know quite well. His position was one of almost unimagined luxury. I was to learn that he was no more "human" than I, and in fact decidedly less. He was loath to risk the loss of his catbird seat through rumored laxness, and so, with the unacknowledged but willing cooperation of the Souls, urged his staff to enforce sterner disciplinary measures.

This lit fuse sparked upon powder on the night of November 14, when a group of suffragists—most of whom had been previously imprisoned and pardoned—were returned to the Workhouse. This undeniable evidence of the failure of incarceration to curb the women's protests was apparently the final straw, and Butler ordered some forty guards to make sure that the new inductees would never again willingly enter the walls under his control. This produced a feast of pain and fear exceeding all that he had never experienced.

It would later, in the memories of the inmates and in the minds of the public who absorbed the many media reports, be known as the "Night of Terror." The guards set upon the women in an orgy of violence. Many prisoners were beaten to unconsciousness, and one woman was stabbed between the eyes with the broken post of her own banner. Concussions, lacerations without number, and broken bones resulted, yet none of those injured received even the most minimal medical assistance, instead being thrown—often limp and unresponsive—into concrete cells.

It is the greatest of frustrations to be a monster, yet be forced by circumstances to keep the qualities that identify that monstrosity hidden. Though my instincts demanded that I defend the brutalized women, and the overriding stench of spilled blood urged me to abandon my disguise, I stubbornly limited myself to defenses which would not call attention to my true nature.

I threw my body atop the supine to absorb blows that would have harmed them more than me and, when possible, captured the will of a guard and sent him against his compatriots as if he had suffered an attack of conscience. It was only when I saw Lucy Burns struggling mightily with her attackers that I was moved to more direct action.

Braving a gauntlet of truncheons to reach her, I stood by the redhead's side. Displaying only a hint of the strength and speed I possessed, I supported her efforts for some moments, to the lasting pain of several of the guards, before she was clubbed from behind and dragged away. At that point I fell to the ground myself in hopes that we would be taken to the same quarters.

It was not to be. Still resisting enough to give credence to my surrender, I soon found myself locked in a barred enclosure, and quite alone. It was apparently in one of a block of cells, and from the cries of those imprisoned near me I was able to gather news of new horrors as the night progressed.

"Oh!" cried one. "They've chained Miss Burns' hands to the top of her bars! Her feet can barely reach the ground! What will become of her?"

And then another, whose voice seemed to be that of Alice Cosu, whom I had met not long before in the F Street office, wailed out. "Miss Lewis has been hurled into a cell." she mourned. "Her head struck the iron bedstead. I fear she has died! Who will have mercy upon us?" At which point this voice stopped with a gasp of pain, and the speaker herself seemed to drop to the floor.

The sounds of struggle from without quickly diminished, followed only by the heavy clanging of additional cells, and the soft moans of the injured. The guards had succeeded in their bloody task, and the recidivist suffragists were one and all subdued and locked away.

I sat awake listening through that entire terrible night. Never did I hear anything like medical assistance being offered to the injured, only the weak cries of exhausted women slipping into sleep despite their pains and the crude and self-congratulatory boasting of their tormentors.

Then another voice sounded, confident and assertive.

"Your work is not done, my boys! I want this blood mopped up straightaway. Leave even a scrap of evidence and you'll rue your incompetence. And there must be no reporting of this night. Close more tightly any avenues of communication with the outside, and let it be known that if I discover any one of these women is responsible for the kind of scurrilous media attention this fine institution has been receiving, she will perish within these walls!"

I had never heard those tones before, but I knew instinctively that it was Butler who spoke, and by the evidence of his voice I suddenly recognized him for what he was. I do not hesitate to confess that I shivered in my lone cell at this discovery, suddenly fearful not only for the suffragists, but for the continued existence of yours truly.

CHAPTER 33

I was certain that his next move would be to tour the cells to celebrate his triumph, and to feast richly on the misery he had caused. I dared not let him recognize me for what I was as I was certain that even were I uncaged, I would not be his match. As I heard the footsteps approaching, I huddled in the corner of my cell, innocuous as a bundle of rags, my eyes to the wall and daring no movement, the unnatural grace of which would surely have given me away.

I heard him as he passed, and if I had needed any additional assurance. I had it here. Oh, the inhuman elegance of his footsteps: precise as the striking of a metronome amongst the ragged gravel toss of those of the guards! I have heard some reckless beings rhapsodize over the joys of facing a worthy opponent; they have not, I assure you, been in the straights I found myself in then.

Though I was not yet old in the ways of the Kin, I had come to recognize the great variety of creatures, some rumored in fantastical fiction, others published nowhere but in nightmare, that share the world with mortal man. I had faced dragons and the great crocodiles that ape their appearance, encountered were-creatures, the self-named spirit of Demosthenes, and the mysterious Souls, but Butler was unique among the creatures that I had encountered.

I shall call him "Demon," if only because I know no better name. As my Kin subsist upon the blood of the living, there are those who thrive upon pain and suffering, fattening upon it as the most indulgent of country squires tucks into an extravagant joint. This was my enemy's nature, and through shrewdness and unnatural patience he had ensconced himself within a monstrous pantry in which he could sip and sup at his leisure. And in it he had grown to a terrible strength.

Even if I had a chance to contest with him one on one without witnesses, I held no delusion as to my chances. As he had revealed his fear of publicity, I determined my role must be to do what I could to release news of the Night of Terror to the outside world. Though caged and weakened (I had supped only lightly since my incarceration, and had spent much of that healing the wounds I received while sheltering others), I was not without weapons, not the least of these being my wits and my unholy determination.

The first step was to collect information. I knew that many of the suffragists made a habit of secreting the stub of a pencil and scraps of paper in their clothing so they would not have to have to resort to memory when recounting the outrages they endured. Though I was imprisoned, my money was not, and I was confident it would find a way to reach me even here.

Butler forbade us even to speak with one another, threatening one inmate in my hearing that he would fit her with a brace and bit and wrap her in a straightjacket if she were to utter even a sound. It was not possible for him to station a man at every cell, however. The guards here grew slovenly when their tasks were not so interesting as brutalizing helpless women, so if we watched for a chance, we found it possible to whisper to those in the adjacent cells. Thus, slowly I admit, messages found their way among us.

In this manner I managed to spread the word that, if information detailing the horrors of our confinement could be brought to me, I would contrive a way to get it to our compatriots outside. Unfortunately, it required some days for this to be collected, simply because it was difficult for many of the prisoners to find privacy enough to scribble their accounts. Lucy, for example, endured additional abuses before being allowed to suffer alone.)

Time was not my friend in this. I grew steadily weaker, and even the rats, which I had used in the past to keep my strength up, proved too wary for my increasingly clumsy efforts at capture. I prepared a simple message, nothing more than a telephone number and the directive to "pay this man for information," and waited.

On my second morning in the cell, a guard came around with a simple breakfast of toast and water. Though he offered no comfort, I thought I detected intelligence, and even compassion, in his dark eyes. I dared the risk and returned the uneaten meal to him with my note atop it. He raised his eyes questioningly upon seeing it, and I found I had energy enough to compel him to slip his wrist through the bars. He was a hard man in an ugly job, and no doubt the hand that reached into my enclosure had been not long before bloodied beating suffragists, but I supped on him, closing the wounds with a lick, and found the repast as sweet as any cream.

I could see him regain control of his will as she shuffled off to offer the meal I had refused to the inmate in the next cell. I was encouraged to see him slip my message into the pocket of his uniform. A guard's pay was not generous, and I dared hope that I had obtained the conduit I sought.

His rounds only took him past my little prison every second day, but when he next appeared I found a missive beneath my toast, assuring me that quick and efficient use would be made of any information I could provide. It was as if I had been thrown into a bear pit and discovered there a spear. Despite the suffering all around me, I allowed myself a smile.

So the days passed, and bit by bit scraps of paper, tossed from one cell to another in the wake of a guard's passing, made it to my floor. I secured these in the most intimate of my underclothing until "my" attendant next made the rounds. I fed from him frugally as needed, and each time secreted my missives beneath my uneaten toast.

I saw no direct evidence of the upshots of these actions. However, Butler himself became a regular presence. One woman after another was taken for private conference with him, to be given a chance to return to the general population or, when she refused (as most did), to be introduced to force feeding and other horrors. Unbeknownst to us all, beyond the walls of the Workhouse a storm was building.

At some point, the Demon must have realized that information was being passed from the inmates to the world outside despite his threats. I'm sure questions regarding this insubordination were among those put to the women he interviewed, but abuse serves only to stiffen the spines of the dedicated, and I doubt he learned anything of substance.

How he must have fed during those days! The Night of Terror had apparently introduced him to pain more succulent than any he had sampled before, and like an addict, his need drove him to seek ever stronger pleasures and in the process overmastered his caution.

I first learned the full extent of his hubris on the morning of the twenty-second, when a lengthier note than usual, rolled up in front of my cell. I immediately recognized the writing as the hand of Lucy Burns, and from its contents was quickly assured that the ferocious redhead was not at all cowed by the treatment she had received. She had managed to compile information in a manner that was not only detailed, but reflected a decidedly literary care. I knew as soon as I read it that my spear had suddenly transformed itself into a rifle. Now it was I who hunted the bear.

CHAPTER 34

Lucy's account was in a small, cramped hand, covering the page from border to border like a dense filigree, paper always being at a premium in that place. It did not describe her chained hanging during the Night of Terror, nor the beatings that preceded it as she had already documented those in earlier missives smuggled to me. The events described therein were more intimate and prosaic, but Miss Burns apparently knew well that it was that very sheen of normalcy that gave her narrative its horror. It was dated at midnight of the twenty-first, just hours before I received it, and she had clearly set to transcribing it while new terrors unfolded just beyond her door. I will reproduce it in its entirety here.

Mrs. Lewis and I were asked to go to the operating room. Went there and found our clothes. Told we were going to go to Washington. No reason as usual. When we were dressed, Dr. Gannon appeared, and said he wished to examine us. Both refused. Were dragged through the halls by force, our clothing partly removed by force, and we were examined, heart tested, blood pressure and pulse taken. Of course such data was of no value after such a struggle. Dr. Gannon told me that I must be fed. Was stretched on bed, two doctors, matron, four colored prisoners present. Butler in hall. I was held down by five people at legs, arms, and head. I refused to open mouth. Gannon pushed tube up left nostril. I turned and twisted my head all I could but he managed to push it up. It hurts nose and throat very much and makes nose bleed freely. Tube drawn out covered with blood. Operation leaves one very sick. Food dumped directly into stomach feels like a ball of lead. Left nostril, throat, and muscles of neck very sore all night. After this I was brought into the hospital in an ambulance. Mrs. Lewis and I placed in the same room. Slept hardly at all. This morning Dr. Ladd appeared with his tube. Mrs. Lewis and I said we would not be forcibly fed. Said he would call in men guards and force us to submit. Sent away and we were not fed at all this morning. We hear them outside now cracking eggs.

"We hear them outside now cracking eggs." How much dread is invoked by those seven simple words! It was almost more than my patience could take to wait for the rounds to bring my now familiar guard around again. Such was my sense of urgency that I even considered raising a row in hopes of bringing him sooner, but sanity prevailed; doing so might have resulted in my being moved and no longer accessible to my designated messenger.

Eventually he arrived, and though we exchanged no words (as it seemed that any conversation with the prisons outside of cursing and abuse was prohibited), I felt I had sensed a growing sympathy in his eyes with each batch of messages smuggled out. I also noted that he had augmented his uniform with a pair of smart and comfortable looking shoes, so I was confident that he was both delivering the material I charged him with, and being rewarded for such efforts as I had intended.

It wasn't long before other evidence attested to the success of my endeavors. Though we were denied any news from without, Butler (who often walked these halls, always causing me to remain silent and inert for fear of alerting him to my nature) became more belligerent still, and abusive to his minions as well as to the suffragists, as if he knew that his gag order was being violated but was unable to pinpoint either how or by whom.

Faced with his anger, the guards responded in a variety of ways. Some became more lenient, as if they sensed the brewing storm, despite the urging of the Souls, and wanted to absolve themselves of responsibility while opportunities offered themselves. Others, reacting more like cornered vermin than humans, only increased their ferocity such that I'm sure many of the suffragists counted their imprisoning bars as protection as well as confinement.

The Souls only shrieked the louder as the number of individuals receptive to their siren songs diminished; each guard who turned toward his own humanity being lost to their army of puppets. Those mysterious entities knew me for what I was and continued to keep their distance, but were unable to whisper this information in Butler's ear.

I remained certain that Lucy Burn's revelations were the crackerjack we needed and that they were already having their influence beyond the Workhouse walls, and information continued to be passed my way. I became so inured to tales of injury and brutality I felt that some of these were not worth reporting. Still, I fastidiously sent each on its way, like an author who dispatches both jewel and dross into the mails, never knowing which will catch the public's eye.

Through the incoming notes, I learned that Alice Paul had been transferred from the Workhouse to the District Jail following the failed attempt to categorize her as insane. There, she maintained her hunger strike. I had no doubt she faced the continued violation of force feeding. This was a more public incarceration, so the jail was not subject to the last letter of Butler's control. News of her brave ordeal was surfacing even as the information I was smuggling out was released to more and more people.

Soon thereafter, I heard an unfamiliar voice accompanying Butler's distinctively inhuman footsteps through our section. The new gentleman I later learned was Dr. John Winters Brannon. He was President of the Board of Trustees of Bellevue and Allied Hospitals of New York, and husband of an imprisoned suffragist. He was remonstrating loudly with the superintendent, who strove to hold his ground to set strict conditions for an interview between the captive Mrs. Brannon and her spouse. This was the first apparent crack in the Occoquan walls, and soon the stain of what had happened within would be visible to all.

CHAPTER 35

Shortly thereafter, the bulk of the prisoners incarcerated in the Workhouse were either transferred to the Washington Asylum Jail, or released. I was one of the latter group, and I can state without shame that I felt real joy to find myself beyond those hateful walls, though the sun was high upon my release and I had to take some rapid measures to cover my poor skin.

Despite that light, which forced me to bundle like an ancient mummy, I made sure to visit a news agent before returning to my rooms and purchased every periodical I could find which contained news of the events at that dreadful facility. These were many, as the suffragists' publicity campaign had been working round the clock. This was fed with the information I'd managed to smuggle out concerning the Night of Terror and subsequent events, as well as news of their own continuing protests and updates on Alice Paul's ongoing hunger strike.

I intended to peruse these in full when in the safely shuttered confines of my hotel, but despite the disruption to my circadian rhythm from my time in the sunless confines of Butler's hell-hole, I fell into a deep sleep immediately upon contact with my familiar bed. It was only with the onset of evening and my awakening that I was able to catch up on the news of the day.

Perhaps most telling was the revelation that the National Women's Party had gone to court to protest the horrors of Occoquan, an action that had likely precipitated the recent transfers and my own release. There was news everywhere, even in the *New York Times* which, as I've elsewhere averred, had long been no friend to suffrage. The revelations of the abuses suffered by these women, many of whom were from the best of families and even politically connected, engendered a widespread outpouring of condemnation; even if some editors opined the victims were misguided and occasionally rash.

When I was sufficiently recovered I saw to my own affairs, and was pleased to discover that, though my involvement with its fortunes had been less intimate in the recent past, my money had continued to multiply itself; so charitable were wartime conditions to the enhancement of fortune and the reputation of investment firms. I made some small adjustments, more for my own satisfaction than from any necessity, before returning my attentions to the other matters at hand.

I was well informed on one of these, at least. Zula Woodhull, by virtue of her infamous surname, had caught the attention of several of the more audacious newspaper columnists. Under the guise of reporting upon her upcoming production, they found opportunity to titillate their readers with tales of Victoria's reckless life and the predictably licentious subject of Woodhull *mere's* beliefs concerning free love. From these accounts, I learned that progress on the play continued apace, with opening night scheduled for not quite two months hence. All accounts seemed to get the date and time correct, and I assume Zula thought it bargain-rate publicity,

I also braved the Medusa of the telephone lines to contact Mamie Clover. I assumed that, given how well-connected she was, she would have heard of my incarceration. This proved to be the case, but I was able to reassure her that it had been quite voluntary, and that there had never been a moment when I wasn't sure I could free myself if I so wished. If the latter was not quite true, I found dissembling through the prophylactic of long-distance wires far more easily accomplished than in person.

The Souls were still in evidence, but even they appeared disheartened by the reversal of fortune their cause had suffered. Oh, they continued to harangue the crowds that gathered each time the Sentinels took up their place at the White House gates, but other than encouraging a few random acts of violence on the part of those most easily manipulated—mostly men made ignorant by drink or birth—their star was clearly falling.

When I was able to visit the suffragists' house I was received warmly for the most part. There were some who felt that by accepting pardon I had proved traitor to those still inside. I was able to pass along some additional details about life in the Workhouse which, though not on their own inflammatory, provided useful embroidery with which to strengthen the verisimilitude of the constant press releases.

It was there I learned that, as a result of the barrage of media coverage and their own ongoing legal actions, it was rumored that all of those still imprisoned would soon be released. Only Alice Paul, perhaps sensing victory, had refused this concession and vowed to maintain her hunger strike until suffrage was granted. When she was later turned out of prison despite her wishes, there was every bit as much anger as relief reflected in her weary face.

So matters continued for some weeks, with a constant infusion of news and rumor. Butler had already faced suspension and reinstatement once during the crisis, was said to have drawn into himself, turtle-like, following the transfer of the difficult woman beyond his reach. It seemed he hoped to ride out the storm in relative invisibility. His name had been inextricably linked to the Night of Terror, however, and every new trumpet blast the media sounded must have shivered the walls he sought to hide behind.

I was happy enough to leave him there for the moment, for, as Mamie would have it, "only a fool tries to trouble a hurt snake." The Souls were weakened, and it would not do to dither and allow them to regain strength. And as far as I had been able to discover, it would only be through the intercession of the spirit Demosthenes that they could be thwarted once and for all.

CHAPTER 36

At the time, I believed my best opportunity to involve the spirit and confound the Souls lay in the work being done by Zula Woodhull. According to the scandal sheets I'd perused, she intended to stage her play at the Sylvan, a newly constructed outdoor theater that was then the pride of the Capital. This was a daring move on her part. Association with the federally funded theater would lend weight to her production, but even in the usually temperate Washington D.C., staging a drama at an outdoor venue in winter was a calculated risk.

Again resorting to the infernal telephone, I discovered she could be found at her lodgings (the hotel's billing an automatic line item in my budget already). Late on the afternoon following my visit to the suffragists, I secured a cab and made my way to the Harrington. Arriving at her rooms, I found a situation quite at odds with the placid setting under which we had conducted our séance.

I had some hint of what was happening while still outside the door. Within, I could hear Miss Woodhull now disclaiming a line, this outburst followed by a groan and the scratching of a pen before she vocalized yet again. My knock interrupted her, and though I suspect she was loath to break from her efforts, she opened the door and bade me enter.

Every horizontal surface was awash in paper. It seemed that Zula shared the misgivings of many authors faced with the presentation of their efforts to the public. What had seemed excellent, even groundbreaking, before, was now apparently in desperate need of repair. She looked up at me with an expression of panic.

"Such shortcomings, Miss Monot!" she exclaimed. "How is it that I did not see them before now, with my cast already chosen and rehearsals to begin?"

I cannot pretend to understand the artistic temperament (and it is not through lack of trying, I assure you), but made what efforts I could to calm her. I assured Zula that it had been the very strengths of her writing that had moved me to fund the project (it seeming that a lie was the best medicine at the time). She calmed somewhat at that, and begin gathering the amended pages together as we continued to speak.

Though the money meant little to me, I thought that bringing a businesslike order to the conversation might be the easiest oil to pour on her troubled creative waters, so I first asked for an accounting of the funds so far spent. I was pleased to find that Zula's involvement in her mother's many enterprises had served her well, for her books were detailed and nigglingly inclusive. She proceeded to explain these item by item, a tad defensively I must say, until I had all that I could stand and waved her quiet.

"Other than the fine tuning of the script, then," I said, "am I to assume that all goes according to schedule, and that we can expect you to give us your play on the date announced?"

This apparently threw her back upon her concerns about the manuscript, for she glanced at the loosely stacked pages before continuing bravely.

"The cast is selected, and a venue secured," she assured me. "And I hope to begin rehearsals soon. There are still props to be found, the set designs to finalize, and costuming. The latter I hope to delay until the last minute, lest one or more of the actors prove unsuitable and sizes change." Here, she paused for a heavy breath. "But to answer your question directly, yes I fully intend to meet the schedule as announced."

"And have you," I asked, "heard anything further from our friend Demosthenes?"

This change of tack took her aback, and she appeared flustered when answering.

"Not since our encounter, no. I see no profit in dealing with that spirit again. He has no love for, or loyalty to me. Indeed, I question whether he would even answer a summons now, particularly without the lure of my mother's hat, which I seem unable to locate."

I only nodded, not wishing to let her know of my loss of that heirloom, and continued to probe gently.

"Ah, I thought perhaps you might have other keepsakes that would prove as useful."

"Not here with me,' she said. "My mother was less than supportive of my theatrical ambitions. In fact her comments upon *Affinities* itself were far from generous. So while I will submit to her name being brought up in relation to my work for the sake of publicity, I purposefully travelled without any links that might invoke that heritage. The hat was accidentally packed, as I had been wearing it since she cast it off."

I was careful to not let my disappointment show, so as not to tip my hand regarding my ulterior motives in this little enterprise, and waved away the topic as if of no interest.

"It was a matter of curiosity, no more," I assured her. "Indeed, I fear you must put all thoughts of such matters aside, as a torn mind is no boon to the creative process. Have my agents been forthcoming with funding as you've required it?"

She assured me that they had. Her continual glances at the stacked papers clearly indicated that she itched to be back to work on her revisions, so I indulged in only enough small talk to make sure the matter of spiritual contact was sufficiently buried before taking my leave. Zula had pen in hand again before I had swung closed the door, already too immersed to answer my farewell.

CHAPTER 37

While the rough beast of Miss Woodhull's *Affinities* took shape in the playwright's mind, the suffragists continued to dominate the news. The media fed upon itself—as is its nature—and soon rumor and innuendo became fact in the public mind. The Night of Terror was seen to be worse than it actually was, though the truth of it was horror enough.

No politician loves bad news, and clearly Wilson was feeling the pressure. It also seemed that Carrie Catt, positioning herself as a safer alternative to Alice Paul, continued to promote her "winning strategy" movement toward a national amendment. She worked within the government to demonstrate that "good women" could move the cause forward as effectively as could "radicals."

For all Mrs. Catt's efforts to steal the limelight, it was Alice Paul's National Women's Party that shaped the national conversation. On November 27 and 28, all of the remaining suffragists, including Miss Paul (who had been incarcerated for five weeks, and as I've said resisted her dismissal till the end) were freed.

All of their arrests and detentions would later be ruled unconstitutional. Rather than crow over this victory, Alice and her compatriots kept up the pressure through both legal action, and continued protests.

As the year turned, the continued publicity bombarding the White House finally took its toll. Facing the specter of protests outside his very gate on a daily basis, and nudged politically from within by Carrie Catt and her ilk, Wilson announced his support for the women's vote in January of 1918. He touted suffrage as a "war measure" that was important to morale within the country, and to the nation's standing in the world. At first, I thought this a victory.

It seemed my understanding of the American political system was less than sophisticated. Not only did such a measure, even with Wilson's support, need to pass successfully through the Senate and Congress, the resulting Congressional Amendment would require the approval of three-quarters of the established states. There was still road aplenty ahead. Alice Paul's suffragists pledged to keep a protesting presence at the White House gates until a woman's right to vote was guaranteed by the law of the land.

In fact, Alice vowed to specifically keep the pressure on President Wilson. To her way of thinking, his party was the one most likely to bring about suffrage, and as the head of the progressive Democrats, blame for their every inaction was his own. The president may have expected something more in the way of acknowledgment for his bold action, and in retaliation for Paul's harassment seemed determined to throw the mantle of success—when it was achieved—upon his "friend" Carrie Chapman Catt.

I must say, however, that Alice Paul may well have been one of those extremely rare individuals for whom the cause outweighs any personal glory. It seemed that suffrage was the row she had pledged to plow, regardless of who was credited when the end was reached.

Wilson's "Fourteen Points" speech, presented early in 1918, served to further provoke the suffragists. For though that document foresaw the end of the war and presented what Wilson obviously saw as a blueprint for a fair and lasting peace, it made no specific mention of the electoral equality issue in America. So even though the women of New York State obtained the vote (and brought millions of active individuals into the political life of the nation), Alice Paul felt compelled to serve notice to the President that her battle was not won.

Though Wilson became the figurehead for any delays in the march toward suffrage, it was the Souls against whom the little brunette most directly struggled. These entities had been briefly subdued by the exposure of the evils of Occoquan and the public support engendered by those revelations, but there was fear enough surrounding the concept of the woman's vote to fuel their resurgence.

Race relations added to the toxic mix of policies proposed and policies prevented. The Southern States, still quietly seething over the loss of the War Between the States, now bent their efforts toward the suppression of the votes of freed slaves. The fear was that were Negro women to receive suffrage, their numbers would create a political earthquake in the South.

Some advocates for the women's vote, including Carrie Catt, even attempted to play on this fear by claiming that the votes of white women could counter those of the freed slaves. In fact, Arkansas passed a peculiar law granting suffrage to only Caucasian women, allowing them to vote in primaries, but not general elections. This shameful posturing accomplished little, though most agreed that if suffrage could be restricted to white women alone it would have passed long ago.

Such political hot-buttons were food and drink to the Souls, and bigotry opened ears eager for the entities' hemlock of hatred. Thus, when the question was brought before the United States House of Representatives, it won only the precise number of votes required. However, the Senate refused to even consider the issue until the following October.

To Alice Paul's eyes, this was clearly a failure of leadership, and the protests against Wilson became more directly antagonistic than ever. Occoquan remained an issue in the eyes of the public as well, and to keep it in the news, the National Women's Party continued their legal action.

Somewhere during this period, and likely partly a result of those efforts in the courts, I heard the gratifying news that Butler had resigned. I dearly hoped that this meant I would not be forced into a confrontation with the creature who still filled me with dread. It was a time of cautious optimism after all, and I expect I proved as susceptible to this mood as any.

CHAPTER 38

The winter of 1917-1918 proved to be one of the coldest the Capital had ever endured. If Zula regretted her impulsive booking of the outdoor National Sylvan Theater I saw no sign of it. Her play was scheduled for the boards, and it would be staged even if the diva needed trussing up until she looked like a polar bear.

In fact, now that the bulk of the money had been spent and the production seemed a *fait accompli,* not to be held back by man nor beast whatever its shortcomings, I discovered an unanticipated vein of optimism in Miss Woodhull. She seemed to have cast off some overwhelming weight or obligation, and I wondered if stepping free of a mother's notorious skirts could indeed prove so liberating.

I remarked on her positive mood, though you can be sure I did so without invoking any of my theories of generational struggle.

Dear Zula took no offence, at any rate.

"The play is mine, and it will see the boards now, and shall stand or fall entirely upon my own abilities."

"So your mother did not assist you in this enterprise?" I asked.

She laughed, seeming quite carefree.

"Oh, as I might have mentioned, she read my manuscript. It still bears the wounds she inflicted. I'll show you them sometime. But I did not incorporate the least of her commas into it." Then, perhaps fearing she had been too honest or too harsh, she amended herself. "It is not that I doubt her genius, but that I cannot allow myself to question my own."

To this I nodded politely, recognizing her modesty but not tacitly agreeing with it. We were a week from opening, and the weather did not look poised for any significant change. It was a safe bet that those in the front rows would be able to see the actors' breath during each exhortation.

"Do you have a script I might borrow?" I asked. "With the premiere so close, I'm sure my enjoyment would be elevated were I able to read the play again before seeing it staged."

Miss Woodhull had been, as I've noted before, cautious with her expenditures. She had not had more copies of the play printed than her cast required, but was able to produce an older version from her luggage that she entrusted to me.

"It is my own original," she admonished me, "pray treat it with care, as I'm sure you will."

I took my leave of her with a promise that I would. It was fast becoming winter, and a harsh one as well, but there was a sense of change in the air in those days as heady as any spring. In such circumstances, it is easy to grow overconfident.

The sides arrayed on the game board still looked equally matched; the suffragists and their determination and sense of destiny facing off against the Souls and their legions of hatred. It was at the first point for which success seemed not only possible, but inevitable. I've since learned that such periods of quicksand are common in history, and I'd like to believe I have grown more facile at avoiding them.

CHAPTER 39

The war was the main act to which all other human activities were as side dramas. As the year ticked over from 1917 to 1918, despite some colorful successes, including the exploits of the marvelously refreshing T.E. Lawrence in Arabia and Palestine, the German Army was far from finished.

Wilson continued to look through the smoke of war toward peace. His "Four Principles" speech in February seemed to anticipate a defeated Germany and to lay the groundwork for a just reconciliation. Perhaps the Kaiser took this as presumption, or perhaps his generals noted that though the American military machine was flexing its muscles, it was doing so slowly enough to have had little influence on the battlefield as yet. For one of these reasons, or both, or neither, Germany was to launch a series of attacks over the months ahead that would prematurely end the war for thousands of young men, regardless of country.

Such international machinations required derivative activity in the world of investments. I was able to do this, but

I confess that anyone with a grubstake who cannot make money in a war—especially when on the side to be victorious —is probably not suited to a life in finance.

An uncertain world, and personal affairs which because of this nag, are ingredients one would wish when whipping up a recipe to create a hunger for entertainment. If she was confounded by the weather, Zula was blessed by other factors. Anticipation for her play began to enter into the talk of the day, that popularity assuring that the media would again bring it to the fore.

The suffragists were not enthralled. Despite Miss Woodhull's surname (or in some cases because of it) she enjoyed no place of pride among the mostly younger women who had picked up the banners her mother had dropped. Many of them seemed to regard theater itself as a frivolous thing, the intellectual meat of the well-to-do housewife and not suited to young women of modern ideas.

I sought to counter this train of thought. It seemed important to me that Zula's staging draw a sizable crowd, and since I was able to offer tickets at no charge, I converted several of the least messianic of Alice's group. Miss Paul was more resistant still. It was only after I had threatened to drag her if she refused that she accepted my invitation; and only then, I think, because she dreaded the thought of a lingering touch more than she feared my victory.

Lucy Burns, on the other hand, agreed to go straightaway. If crowds were in the offing and the price was right, the redhead was never one to avoid adventure. She was also something of an historian of her enthusiasms, and thus more knowledgeable concerning Woodhull *mere* than were many of her sisters. I vowed to keep them both close to me, as I was quite unsure what forces Zula's little comedy of manners might release.

When opening night finally arrived and we reached the theater, it was immediately clear that my efforts to inflate attendance had been unnecessary. In fact, the entire amphitheater was mobbed with patrons. It was also apparent that the crowd might not have been the audience poor Zula had dreamed of. It was largely a male gathering, more likely lured in hopes of seeing (and shouting down) something scandalous *a la* Victoria than through any interest in the daughter's dramaturgy. These were accompanied by an almost equal number of Souls, which did nothing to dampen my apprehension.

Despite the chill, there was also a taint of rotten vegetables on the air, proof that at least one of these would-be critics planned to sign his rant dramatically. The play had not yet begun, but the audience was past ripe for throwing.

Faced with the reality of the event, and one seemingly primed to go very wrong, I had to admit that my plans were again flimsy to the point of foolishness. They depended upon chance such that the riflewoman whom I once was, who had chased control until the very break of the trigger would fend shocking. My initial plot had required having the hat, which seemed to exert some sort of hold over Demosthenes.

Without the heirloom, I was reduced to hoping the spirit had enough family loyalty, or ethereal curiosity, to be drawn to Zula's big event. If so, I might remonstrate with it on behalf of the suffragists. You may rest assured that the scheme had not seemed so harebrained until examined in the light of immediacy. I scanned my surroundings, but though the area was chock-a-block with mortals and Souls, there was no sign of Victoria's spirit guide.

CHAPTER 40

Zula had clearly done some rewriting in anticipation of her chilly stage, as the play opened not in a drawing room as the original had, but in a hall. There the scientist/ protagonist/love interest "Teslett" has demanded that every window be thrown open to permit access to "the wild energy of the air" or some such claptrap. This genius clearly has an influence upon Lady Olga who, quite overcome by a bipartite intoxication of both science and a dramatic background of music, declares her love for Teslett.

The play held its audience's interest to this point, and I'm sure some of the attendees were fairly licking their lips at the declaration, certain that something scandalous was to come. It was not to be, however. Despite the fact that some of the ideas it espoused were rather controversial, *Affinities* explored them in language that—to this American ear, at least—seemed stilted and almost antique. That coupled with a restlessness born of the growing cold and the urging of the Souls, nudged the audience ever closer to action.

It was a near thing. The actors and actresses Miss Woodhull had chosen were enthusiastic and well directed. Miss Marie Dainton in particular, who played Lady Olga, was a revelation. She tackled the role with a clear, operatic voice, and a presence that was innocent and otherworldly by turns. The earnestness of these players, and even the innocence of the play, which steered well clear of the sort of scandal many had been expecting, kept the crowd in hand for some time.

I continued to sift through the gathering, hoping against hope for sight of Demosthenes. I was close enough to observe the event that ended all restraint, yet helpless to prevent it. A gentleman who was well into his cups had fallen asleep, but started awake and—clearly unaware of his location—shouted out in a panicked slur.

"Whut's all this? Whar' t'Hell am I?"

A ringing silence followed this outburst; even the actors on the stage paused to try to locate the source of the disturbance. And then another wit, clearly thinking this the cleverest retort of the season, called out the same.

"Whut's all this? Whar' t'Hell am I?"

The audience fell into laugher. From that point on it only took another sport repeating the drunkard's call to kindle hilarity anew. The actors struggled heroically, declaiming all the louder to be heard over the cackles and catcalls. The constant interruption soon caused the players to wander about the script and, quite lost myself, I fished in my purse for the copy Miss Woodhull had entrusted to me.

A limp stalk of carrot hit the stage (the more commonly thrown produce in short supply in winter and a war economy) as I flipped through the loosely bound pages as if by locating the correct spot in the script I could somehow follow the performance. The Souls were merciless now, having driven their hosts to the brink of violence, they wished them over that border.

Recognizing the growing danger, I sent my companions back to a safe distance (to Alice's relief and Lucy's consternation). I then began to consider how I might protect the players and Miss Woodhull, who surely sat behind the curtains, should worse come to worst. Then, glancing to the stage and back again to the papers in my hand, I noticed a scrap of handwriting circling the border of the page.

I did not recognize the hand, though I later noticed that it was quite distinctive) but the words there penned were clear enough.

"My dear Zulu," it said, "there is too much polemic here. You must also give them the senses!"

More vegetables flew, and men were jumping to their feet as they yelled. I flipped a few pages further. The annotations continued with a blessedly maternal regularity. The crowd was tending toward violence, and the formerly repeated catcall was now replaced with curses and disdain cast upon the Woodhull family name. Grabbing at the first penned phrase I came upon, I threw my own voice into the storm.

"My own sweet Zu," I shouted, "surely you can see how wooden all this is!"

It might have been my woman's voice—seemingly alone in a sea of male acrimony—or the strangeness of the words that I uttered, but it was far more likely the blurred vortex of disturbed space appearing suddenly in front on me that stopped the crowd. The materialization advanced and retreated in little, cyclonic half steps. When I felt it slipping too far away, I turned a page and read again, this time in a normal speaking voice.

"Proofread, Zu! Proofread!"

It snapped back as if a leash had been jerked. All around us was silence, as if the world had paused between the halves of a thunderclap to await this conversation. I was relentless, and flipped another few pages and read in a whisper.

"You have learned speechifying from me, and learned it well; but even at her current age Aunt Tennie could teach you much about the arts of persuasion."

As I drew my lips back on the last word, Demosthenes filled the space that had moments before seemed a turbulence of time itself.

"It is her voice," the spirit said, gone soft with wonder.

In reply, I simply flipped through the pages. Victoria had been a thorough editor, and at times as chatty as a sister. There were dozens of notes on the pages, from the professorial to the playful. The spirit's eyes followed, lingering upon each even as the next page covered it. I know something of needs, mortal and not, but I hope never to know the desperation to possess that I saw in those inhuman eyes. I am no stranger to cruelty, but I felt the smallest twinge of pity as I closed the book in front of him.

"It is her voice," Demosthenes repeated, as if through hearing it again, I might glean the import of the sentence.

Clearly, I had chanced onto something most powerful. I tucked the script back in my bag.

"And I have it," I said, hoping to tease out more information.

The spirit's eyes remained fixed upon my purse, as if he could not believe what I had done.

"But it is her voice," he repeated again.

"What does it signify to you?" I asked, opening the clasp just enough for Demosthenes to peer in.

He clearly despaired at my stupidity.

"She wrote those notes in her own hand," Demosthenes explained. "When I read them I can hear her as if she spoke them aloud to me. It is the closest glimpse of her I've had since she deserted me."

The scene around us remained frozen. Though I'd had some had little truck with spirits prior to this encounter, I did not know if I was suffering an illusion or if time had indeed paused while we settled this difference. What choice had I but to soldier on?

"You have two options, Demosthenes," I began, clasping the purse shut again. "I can give you this script, and you will have your dear Victoria's voice with you for all time. Or I can burn it and she will be lost to you forever."

Oh, he wailed, so loudly that I could scarce believe that only I heard. It was clear to me that one choice alone would be palatable to the spirit.

"You must give it to me," he pleaded.

"Perhaps I shall," I said, swinging the purse coyly. "But if I do, you know what I want in return?"

He seethed in frustration, his form stretching high like a guttering candle, but when he regained his normal size and form he spoke with resignation.

"You wish an end to the things that call themselves Souls, and for an end to all meddling of the supernatural in the cause of suffrage."

"No more and no less," I replied.

He stared at the bag. Lost love, drugs, greed, blood; I'd felt the compulsion of them all, but had never tasted debasement like that overcoming the creature who stood before me.

"Very well," Demosthenes boomed, "it shall be as you wish."

I was unsure how the exchange would take place, and was already plotting how I might make certain my wishes were met before the book was in spiritual possession. But apparently the agreement was enough. Without preamble, the script was out of my purse and hands, Demosthenes had shrunk to the size as a lazy dust-devil stirring up a desultory dusting of snow as he spun to nothing, and when I looked around there was not a Soul to be seen. The last of these, my bowler-hatted antagonist from before, made to leap at me, a creature made of pure rage. Then with an expression of surprise, burst like a bubble on a fetid pond and was gone.

The audience, so close to dire acts, now looked around as if lost. Half of them were on their feet, but the anger that had forced them to rise was gone. On the stage, Miss Dainton read the situation with an expert eye, and treated the crowd to an elaborate bow as if closing out a scene.

The onlookers grasped at the piece of normalcy as if it was a life preserver, and a startled few did the only thing they could think to do; they applauded. This was quickly picked up by the crowd, and the players—regardless of where they might have been in the script—retreated to prepare for the final act beneath a veritable thunderstorm of approval.

The crowd was clearly relieved to find matters back on an even keel, and rewarded the final act more than they had the truncated material before. It is safe to say that the opening night of Zula Maud Woodhull's venture into the theater without the benefit of her mother's coattails was nothing less than a triumph. The cast returned for a pair of ovations, and Miss Dainton, as the Lady Olga whose *affinities* for science and music brought her to love and passion, was clearly the woman of the hour.

I shook every hand, rewarded the divine Dainton with a kiss that clearly transcended the collegial (and was pleased to note that she both understood my intent and responded to it), and finally found myself in the company of the playwright herself. Zula was quite over the moon, and recognizing this, I could only admire her attempts at calm. She accepted congratulations as if they were her due—which they certainly were—and was already eagerly imagining openings in other venues in other cities, and the career that such success could spawn.

It was not to be. *Affinities* enjoyed strong attendance on its second night, ticket sales no doubt driven by reports of the ecstatic premiere. But attendance dropped precipitously thereafter, and the production closed. Still, the successful opening seemed enough to carry Zula through the disappointment that followed.

On the other hand, without the pernicious influence of the Souls, the path toward suffrage was dramatically smoothed.

I also collected a personal reward following the wreckage of the play; that prize was to expose me to the greatest threat of my already eventful life.

It was Marie Dainton, of course. She was the bon-bon I'd selected as my reward for good deeds done. Those who know me well know my weakness for talent and beauty. She was perhaps a little old for me (or for me as I appeared), but there is an ageless glamour that the arts confer on some, even as they so efficiently steal from all who labor for them.

A life in drama also almost guaranteed that she had encountered lovers of her own sex before, and that she didn't share the silly exclusion of half of the world's partners for reasons of gender. Finally, I find I have a strange affinity with those lost in theater, song, and dance. Though their professional lives are so very short, and my existence virtually limitless, we cling to our obsessions with an almost equal ferocity.

And 'obsession' might not be too far from the mark. After our first interlude, we remained abed for some fourteen hours. (We did sleep. Neither of us was tireless, after all.) There were simply so many things she'd learned over the years that she wanted to teach me, and I prided myself in giving her a few surprises as well. When we separated, I think we were both comfortably certain that we had more than enough material for a three-act play.

Such dramas we staged! Among our favorites was "the older woman's seduction of the young doxie." Pretty Marie discovered hidden wells of darkness in this roll, and I can assure you that my debutante character, once awakened, was equal to anything her mistress had to offer.

This play presented numerous opportunities for ad-libbing. At some point or another, Marie would be forced to disrobe me. On one particular night I decided to struggle against this assault to add a soupcon of violence to the heady stew we were preparing.

My lover was aware of my strength by then, though she had never questioned it. (You see what I mean about people in the arts?) She chose this instance to resist my efforts which produced a tight wince and a little "ooooooh" of pain.

It would not have been the first time I left an inamorata bruised or strained, but I remembered our trysts in exquisite detail. I have a mental library, you see, and save them all for future perusal. Wouldn't you love to visit? However, nothing Marie and I had done together should have produced such tenderness in that exact spot.

I asked to see, and Marie showed me. This soon lead us into a familiar variation (in which the student, now fully awakened, beguiles her teacher), and the moment was lost. Despite my developing preoccupations, I was able to discern no bruising in the area that had triggered Marie's wince, and recognized that the injury must be deep, and perhaps expertly administered.

I did not pursue the subject. I did not think the damage permanent, and our relationship was free and I cared not a fig if she had other lovers as long as she answered my summons when called upon. This she always seemed eager to do.

Until the night that she didn't. I took it upon myself, in a bit of a huff, to travel to her apartment to discover why. I knocked and called out when I heard her moving within.

"Paulette?" she said. "Oh my dear, I overslept! You must forgive me. Give me just a moment and I'll be all yours."

Under more usual circumstances, I would have remained without as instructed, confident that she would never force me to wait overlong. On this occasion, however, I turned the knob and finding the door unlatched, stepped in.

Most of those in the arts are comfortable among dishabille, and Marie's apartment was no worse than others

I've visited. There was a light snowfall of clothing coating the floor, as befits a woman who might occasionally have to take a sniff before deciding if an item was clean enough to wear. Her vanity table could have belonged to a mad alchemist, it was so cluttered with vial and jar of every description. I expected these things, but the hitches and hesitations I saw as she attempted to hurry into an appropriate outfit were quite another matter.

Approaching Marie, I took her chin in my hand and raised her head, in what had become a pantomime of ours to indicate matters of importance.

"I have never pried, sweet darling," I said, "but you are hurt in places where I cannot have so injured you. If you have found a crueler lover who lures you from me, simply tell me so. I have heard worse before and will again. If this is a matter you wish me to know more about, however, now would be the time to tell all."

She ducked her pretty dark head, and I was certain I saw a quick blush decorate her cheeks (but can I say for sure she was not acting? I certainly did not know the ends of her craft).

"I met him just after the play closed," she said. "He was dressed swell, kind of a toff. Anyway, I figured he'd have money."

I rolled my eyes; I knew I kept Marie well enough, but understood also that an actress must always have an eye out for chance.

"And?" I said.

"Well he was," she said, "rich I mean. At least he took me to nice places and tipped big. Then I began to notice the same pieces of clothing showing up in his outfit in different combinations. You know, not shabby, just seen-before. And all this time he seemed to be getting weaker, like from some disease or other."

"And?" I repeated, not as gently as I might have.

"It was I guess toward the end of the second week when he asked if he could hurt me. He said it wouldn't be anything permanent and that he'd reward me richly if I'd only be a good girl in this matter." She glanced at me. "So I said yes. Of course I did. And this man, this Billy, he found two hard spots under my arms and he pinched them something terrible. Lord, it was like a toothache in my brain. Over and over he did it until I feigned a faint to make it stop. Billy was grateful, and generous, and he really did look better afterward, too.

"After that it was the only thing he wanted. He got real greedy about it. After you noticed me hurting the other night I determined to break it off. Billy didn't want to. Twice he talked me into trusting him, but all he wanted was the harming, so I finally put my foot down. That was last night. He showed up here when I was getting ready to meet you. He hurt me for a long time, Paulette."

I was probably as angry at Marie as I was sympathetic, but I pride myself on being able to hold my own in an improvised scene with anyone.

"You poor dear," I said, casting my senses around the small room, recognizing that it would be a fine moment for a villain's surprise. This done and my caution soothed, I continued. "And might I assume this is a situation in which you would welcome my assistance?"

Marie nodded prettily, and in the dark of my imagination, I could picture her affirming the same to my rival with equal verisimilitude. It was too late, though. I could not keep the question back.

"So what is it you'd have me do?" I asked.

CHAPTER 41

Her request was both less and more than I had expected. My first guess would have been that she wanted me to kill him; as I've said, she'd seen hints of my strength; and is not death the ultimate drama?

"If you could just talk to him," she said. "Get him to leave me alone."

Still holding her face, I gave a quick, hard squeeze before releasing her to remind my lover that I was capable of cruelties as yet untested.

"Think well, my darling, and answer carefully," I said, my eyes hard upon her. "Is this 'Billy' more than human?"

"I'm not sure," she said, with a flirtatious glance. "It's not like I know everything that I probably should…"

So the vixen thought to draw me out! I confess, I found her boldness as appealing as her beauty.

"Tell me what you know, dear Marie," I answered, entering easily into the dance. "There will be time for your questions later."

Accepting for the moment that this was as much as she would get from me, the lithe brunette moved to her vanity and began the final stages of her transformation as she talked.

"At first he was sickly, like I said, and took me as a man does, though roughly. But once I let him hurt me it's like his interest in everything else I can do just vanished. And he got stronger every time he did that. That's the weirdest part."

By now my suspicions had been aroused, and I asked the next question with all the eagerness with which one would answer a four a.m. telephone call.

"I see," I said. "So does your Mr. Billy have a last name?"

"Butler," she said. "His name is Bill Butler."

Though I had half expected the name, sit still went through me like electric shock.

"Come," I said, seizing her arm, "we must go." I dragged Marie from her vanity, her transformation incomplete. It is a tribute to her craft—and perhaps my besottedness)—that I could not say if it were 20 percent or 40 percent or 80percent finished, and I still found her quite lovely.

We bustled out of the apartment, Marie burdened by the only bag I'd allowed her. Fortune was with us: there were a few cabs loitering outside her building. I hired one, and once the door was shut against prying eyes, directed the cabbie onto a route that I hoped would be long enough to allow me time to collect my thoughts.

There are times when the Fates seem to have built up such a momentum that certain events are impossible to avoid. As I dragged out options, each in turn, for study, I had the uncanny feeling that Butler had done the same, and foresaw the only possible ending.

Shouting at the cabby against the chilly air, I bade him turn round and make for my hotel.

CHAPTER 42

I am not a believer in coincidence. I realized that, in all likelihood, Butler had taken up with Marie with full knowledge that she and I were involved. There was every chance that he had detected what he could not see, and determined that only an inhuman power could so rudely topple him from the aerie he had so carefully constructed. He must have sorted through the possibilities and eventually come upon me.

It could also be that it was all happenstance, and Butler only waited (for I had no doubt that he did wait) for what he assumed would be a mortal rival whose pain could fatten him. It was a pretty thought, but I would have been a fool to count upon it.

And what of Marie? How much did she guess concerning my nature and his, and what profit did she seek in this confrontation? She grew quiet as the cab approached my apartment, but her face took on the flushed greed of a girl about to be fought over.

I was fond of the woman, make no mistake, but I hoped she knew me well enough to know that should her well-being threaten my existence, my choice would be easily and rapidly made. I considered broaching a strategy during our final minutes in the cab, but was uncertain whether my advantage would be best advanced by confiding in her or manipulating her, and eventually resigned myself to doing neither.

When we arrived at the building I was rewarded for my patience. I detected a slight increase in my lover's body temperature and an elevation in her respiration. These were mileposts that I had long used when bringing her pleasure and thus easy for me to note; more important, they eliminated any doubt I might have had that Marie knew something of what awaited us within.

I was not surprised to find my door unlocked, but still hesitated before entering. As I listened intently for any sound of a presence from the room. I heard none; such niceties as breathing were only play-acting for the creature inside. I carefully slipped off my gloves and glasses and pocketed them. It would not do to enter this lair unarmed.

Marie showed no such hesitation, and was through ahead of me as soon as I'd freed the latch. I followed her in, careful to shut the door behind me. This was probably unnecessary, as I was fairly certain that no one would be allowed to flee this room. Seated in my most comfortable chair, all at ease like a squire just back from a successful day at the track, waited the monster.

"I knew it," he said, rising. "I *knew* it. I told myself, 'there's a finger in the pie you're not seeing, young fellow me lad,' and, of course, I was right. And then at the Woodhull play, I saw what happened, and I saw you *move*. And now you're here to fight me for what poor scraps of honor Miss Dainton still maintains. It is really quite a lovely gesture."

I had heard his voice before, but it was subtly changed. In the Workhouse, he had been lord and master, reveling in a security that had required years to assemble around him. Here, he was less—though I did not know by how much—and his tones lacked the brute authority they had once exhibited. Now, his voice was quite pleasant to the ear, without any manifest undercurrent of evil.

As he stood, I noted that he moved easily. His clothing, as Marie had mentioned, was no longer as swank at it had been and showed signs of regular use. The pain he had put Miss Dainton through had clearly benefitted him; there was a rude vigor about the creature that I did not know how to plumb.

My lover had entered ahead of me, and stood just to my fore. As she turned to look at me, her lovely face full of expectation, I placed my hand onto the small of her back and thrust her forward into the room, speaking as I did so.

"We have no conflict, creature," I said, with as much implied threat as I dared. "I claim no hold on the woman. Take her as a gift, strengthen yourself, and only pledge that I need not encounter you again."

Despite her endless trips across the boards, the combination of a long dress and a sudden push proved too much for Marie Dainton, and she fell to the polished floor in quite a pretty tumble, her eyes turning to Butler in shock.

He quite ignored her and took a step in my direction.

"No, I don't think so," he said. "You can't buy your freedom with something I already have, something I've already had, when there will be so much more nourishment in your pain, my dear."

His nonchalance very much frightened me. I held my place, frantically running through my armory of abilities to come up with something that would buy more than a short delay.

"You are weakened." I tried to make it conversational, as the thing stepped forward again, coming between Marie and me now.

"Yes, yes I am," he said, smiling ruefully, "but strong enough still, although I've been half starving in feeding upon a woman who has difficulty recalling the last time she had a completely honest feeling."

I could see Marie over his shoulder, while he simply ignored her. She had been stricken by his betrayal and mine, but she positively blanched at the Demon's last statement. I thought she might faint, but unfortunately I had more urgent matters to attend to.

"So," he said, taking another step, a companionable smile on his face, "might I know more of my benefactor?"

I let my teeth drop, for all the good I expected of them, and my words were slurred as a result. I had no thought in my mind beyond selling myself dearly and quickly, to limit the pain he could leech upon.

"I am Paulette Monot," I said, "and may it be the last name you ever hear."

He continued forward as if confident that he could simply walk through whatever defense I might offer.

CHAPTER 43

He might have done, too. Behind him Marie turned into the shadows. When she next appeared she was no longer pale but bright with anger, and she carried the great brass winding key for my old Coilcycle. She raised this heavy weapon above her head and, with the scream "I shall feel *this*, I promise you!" brought it down upon the Demon's crown.

The skull beneath that blow crushed and spread, the ongoing force of the impact sending a wet splash of whatever the bone had once shielded onto the floor.

Very nearly in a panic, I grabbed the girl's hand and fled. Perhaps the sheer physical damage would be a shock, perhaps the key's cruciform shape might have exacerbated the harm done. But one does not kill such things as Butler, one simply tries to make oneself not worth their bother.

If the veldt is full of helpless creatures, why would the lion attack a thing with horns that, though unlikely to kill the predator, can cause it real harm? As a general rule, it is always best to be a thing with horns. With a world full of victims, why would Butler return to two who had hurt him? This wisdom has worked for me so far, but I still keep an eye over my shoulder.

I managed to get Marie to safety. Other than the few hurried words we needed to exchange during that flight, and the necessary formalities some months later when I purchased a townhouse for her, she has never spoken to me again. I've often wondered what I might have lost when she saved me, and I've quite forgiven her.

It was a week before I dared return to my rooms. When I did, I found them just as I'd expected; with the door neatly closed and not locked, the winding key upon the floor, and not the slightest trace of a stain anywhere. I moved soon thereafter. It seemed time.

With an end to supernatural interference, the suffragists swept all before them; though to them it must have seemed a very slow sweep. Their bill failed to pass the Senate as predicted, but Alice's troops merely focused their efforts upon defeating anti-suffrage candidates that autumn. The new Senate passed the bill and, in August of 1920. The deciding vote is said to have been changed by a telegram from a politician's mother. Thus, the Nineteenth Amendment was ratified, fittingly, in Tennessee.

Carrie Chapman Catt was pleased to be recognized as the woman who brought the vote to her gender, and Wilson seemed to take a bullied-boy's vengeance against Alice Paul in recognizing Catt.

Alice Paul never saw an achievement as a finish line but as another step up a seemingly endless staircase. She left the set of Zula's play with nary a question despite the wonders that there occurred, and set to work crafting a document which would prohibit the denial or abridgement of any constitutional right by any state on account of sex. That she would resort to any sort of theater to accomplish her goals I did not doubt. She finished drafting the Equal Rights Amendment in 1923, and died without seeing it ratified. And thus, do the mayflies make progress.

My time with the suffragists was at an end. I was pleased with their accomplishments. I could only see it as a step towards ultimate good: that virtually half of the population of America would now have a voice in making the laws that bound them.

In my dealings with these women, I had always been motivated by curiosity rather than conviction. With the former satisfied, I turned my attention anew to my own place in the world, and to strategies that would ever move it toward the more pleasant and increasingly secure. In this arena, I had gained wisdom as a result of my encounters with Card and—especially—Butler, though the latter had made me visible to an enemy whose attention I would prefer to have never attracted.

Still and all, I'd learned once again—and profited almost by chance—by taking a peek beneath the rocks of mortal society. The more I did so, the more I discovered about other things that coexist with, and prey upon, the warm. The number and variety of such beings no longer surprises me, and that in itself is another layer of armor against the weapons wielded by the unknown.

I have learned that a well-considered existence requires not a balancing between two worlds, but maintaining a perch atop or among many. This seems to be the strategy that the oldest of things employ. I expect to emulate, and eventually join, them. They would be well advised to make room for me.

202

THE END

BRUCE WOODS

MOSTLY IN MY OWN WORDS

If you've perused my three novels, Royal Blood, Dragon Blood, *and* American Blood, *you'll be familiar with my reminiscences about a trio of important periods of modern history. Please be aware that I'm not claiming any important role in these instances. On the contrary, it's likely that they would have all ended as they did without any participation on the part of yours truly. I have only recounted them as remembered, often with the singular assistance of my recordings and notes.*

Upon looking over these screeds with the invaluable assistance of hindsight, I've begun to see them as only our Elders can, in the context of my own development. The longer one lives, it seems, the more themes begin to appear in our undertakings. So as I prepare to leave any further ruminations to those who come after me (should they discover their own voices), I've succumbed to revisiting my own past, particularly as a creature so caught up in mythology as to be often seen as imaginary, in a search for context.

With that in mind, it occurs to me that I've never revealed in print the earliest days after my "making," and how those events set me on the roads I've since travelled. I hope that these notes, imperfect as they are, might set the

*stage as it were, and like a snake eating its own tail,
illustrate that beginnings and endings are arbitrary at best.
The seeds of what I've become were sown in my earliest
days.*

Make of that what you will.

"Shit" was the first word I heard.

It was accented, and the easy phonetic spelling—which
most, I fear, would have succumbed to—would be "shee-it."
But that's not quite right, and as those who know me expect,
I strive for accuracy. I had not yet obtained my Tessier-
Ashpool recording device, so this reconstruction is based
solely on my memory (quite good, thank you) and notes I
scribbled down after the fact,

Perhaps "shuh-eet" would be closer to the truth. At any
rate, it was apparently in reference to my humble apartment,
or to my own appearance, which was certainly not my best.

The speaker, who gradually came into focus, was pinning
me by my shoulders to the bed I'd collapsed on after my
unplanned conversion and the haphazard cleaning
performed by my inadvertent maker. Oh, she was clearly one
of the undead, but her skin, a result of what I assumed was
long exposure to near constant winds, was yellow-pale and
appeared thicker than mine, the fine down on her forearms
seemed quite white in contrast.

Drawn back into a pair of tight pigtails, the hair on her
head was pale as well, as faintly golden as a desiccated
autumn pasture. Her face was extravagantly freckled, and
her eyes, though the lids hooded them, were a brilliant blue.

Temporarily releasing my left shoulder, she struck me across the face with a hard little fist. It was not a glancing blow. I could feel bone break, and I spat out a tooth. It was only as I swallowed my own unfamiliar blood, somehow knowing that it offered strength that I might need, that my assailant nodded in approval and spoke again.

"First lesson," she said, "it will always hurt, and you will always heal. You must remember though, that it will always hurt."

I could feel the bones knitting, and yes the black wash of pain. The hole where the lost tooth had been beat like a drum as I tried to focus on the blue of her eyes. She made no attempt to dominate me; as helpless as I was, it would have been a waste of energy. Holding my focus on her against the pain, with my mouth a mending ruin, I forced the words, each syllable an agony, past a growing tooth. I was clearly overpowered, but that has never stopped me. I husbanded what strength I had for retaliation, though my peripheral vision told me that she was not alone.

"Who are you?" I asked.

"My name is Mamie Clover," she said. "And if I had not taken your part, you would have been disappeared by now. No trace. Nothing. It can still happen, of course."

Her moniker was unlikely, but I instinctively knew that any questions as to how and how long she'd lived would be presumptuous, impertinent, and left unanswered. This was an old one, at least by my lights. I merely repeated her name back to her; somehow pleased that the ongoing mending clarified my speech. Eventually, I formed a question.

"You say you have 'taken my part.' What am I to assume that means?"

She pinned my shoulder with her free hand again, and spoke.

"Your conversion was, to put it politely, unconventional. There are those who oppose any unplanned increase in our numbers, but I decided to examine you myself before allowing their cruelty to hold sway."

"Whatever has happened to me, I did not welcome it." I said. "All it has brought me is terror and hunger, Perhaps the empty sleep of death would be welcome."

"So you made no effort to circumvent the rules," she said. "Intentional or no, you've answered my first question correctly." She stood, releasing me with a nonchalance that I admit chafed me.

"What of the man who tried to kill me, and the other who accidentally made me into whatever I now am?" I asked.

"They have attempted to flee retribution, of course" she said. "The first with a canny cowardice, the second, after tending to you after a fashion, scrambled off in mewling fear. Both have been counseled, and I believe you need not concern yourself with either for the time being."

"It seems the former has shamed himself in more ways than one," I said. "No man should take that which isn't first offered."

She laughed. It was raw and loud and honest.

"You are no rudely plucked blossom, Miss Monot. I know you've given yourself freely when it brought you pleasure or position. It is you, not they, who is on trial here. First, however, I suspect you find yourself peckish?"

At this, one of her compatriots escorted a youth from the shaded edge of the room. He was quite lovely, perhaps a year or two younger than I. He seemed under some sort of a trance, as he advanced with the careful steps of the sleepwalker.

The hunger, which until then had kept up a background murmur, screamed to the fore. I leapt from the bed and started toward him, the still unfamiliar extension of my teeth already underway.

Mamie Clover stopped me and held me back with apparent ease.

"Comfort him," she whispered. "He appears confused."

I gathered the poor boy in my arms, and intended to bestow no more than sisterly kisses on his cheek to better revive him, but suddenly found my risen teeth deep in his neck. Immediately, I felt the great drumbeat of his heart, thrilling me from head to toe, a metronome for the mad erotic dance of the feed. I clove to him, tight as a leech, ready to ride that rhythm to his death.

He would have died in my arms, all willing, had not Mamie Clover torn me easily away despite my struggles.

"Lesson two," she said. "Kill only when you need to. Otherwise, feed daintily and leave no trace. When the African Masai bleed an ox for sustenance, they take only what they need and then free the animal to pasture, where it can recover before it is called upon again. Make that, rather than the elephant who uproots a tree only to sup on the tender upper branches, your model."

Though my mind buzzed like a nest of hornets, I managed to nod. Slowly, I came to realize that I was sated, my stomach distended like an old alcoholic's. Imprisoned in her arms, madness fell from me like autumn leaves in a gust of wind, and I nodded once again.

"Very nice," she said. "Your will is strong. I find myself almost liking you."

When drowning, one will grasp at a limb too slight to offer support, and I did so then.

"Both men and women have found me comely," I said. Though my savior had dressed me, I was far from my full, meticulously decorated beauty, but I straightened my raiment and flirted as well as I could.

Clover laughed again, and there was both surprise and humor in it, before freeing me and sending me flying across the room with a casual, backhanded slap.

"When one weapon is futile, you are quick to try another," she said. "It will not avail you here, but I'd have been disappointed if you hadn't made the attempt."

I stood, the blush that bloomed unbidden attesting to my newborn's lack of control.

Confused and frustrated, I felt tears budding at the corners of my eyes, and knuckled them away. I looked down at my hands, and they were pink with the fruits of my bloody sorrow. It was too much, and I collapsed into blubbering.

"I don't understand." I said, gasping out the words. "I don't know what's happening to me."

It was a strategic retreat of sorts, but I was ever watchful for any weakness that I could exploit.

Mamie Clover stepped closer, and I involuntarily flinched, expecting another attack.

Instead, she only smiled, a wistful little lift of the corners of her lips.

"Oh," she said, "a clever girl like you will figure it out shortly."

Her concept of time was different than that of most and as I was to learn, so was mine. She had much to teach me, and her standing among the Kin hinged upon my learning well. It may have been an afterthought to her, but my continued existence was also in play.

Mamie Clover must have had some correspondence with her American peers about my status, and, I would later learn with Kindred overseas as well. Nothing happened rapidly, however. She aged more slowly than trees, and even my destruction held no urgency for her. So with the first two rules cemented in my mind: I would always heal, but I would always hurt; and I must only kill when necessary, and then do it quickly. With my rent covered for some months ahead, she took me to her home in Kansas.

I'd long been a city girl; my horizons short, the tunnels of streets narrow beneath the looming buildings. We travelled by train, and mostly at night, but in the twilight and dawn I saw enough of the great prairies to leave me terribly frightened. Such endless space with nowhere to hide! I felt a visceral mammalian fear. There was no cover in those open spaces. I was a mouse beneath the bowl of a predatory sky.

My champion was long inured to such discomfort. She knew, as I would have to discover, that there was nothing on that endless plain or in the overarching air more terrible than she. "A clever girl" like me can, it seems, learn lessons even when they're not spoken aloud.

We eventually arrived at Mamie's dwelling, which she shared with her compatriot, Mark. Whether they were husband and wife or brother and sister or both was beyond my ken, and certainly not a question I would have asked. I'm sure tongues wagged concerning their relationship in the prairie town though, where gossip was among the most popular of participatory sports. What I came to know, and the locals did not, is that the couple had managed the affairs of the Kin in the great center of the country, manipulating media and finance as required for quite some time.

The building sat between the river and the foothills, making Mamie and Mark neither waterfront "rabbits" nor upland "goats," as the locals would have it. It was simple enough to avoid undue attention, yet stately enough to command respect. It seemed there were lessons to be learned everywhere.

My personal quarters were in the basement, which was not the dungeon one might expect. Most of the original dwellings in the area were, because of a lack of local timber, simply dug into the earth and covered with sod. One of these formed the basis for my cellar. It is not unlikely that it had been the house that they settled in when Mark and Mamie, then under different identities, first occupied the territory. Being earth-sheltered, the basement apartments were also cool in the summer's heat—though temperature mattered little to me—and easy to keep warm in winter. More important, my rooms tended toward the dark without supplemental lighting, and provided quiet places to contemplate my changing status.

Clover had other tasks at hand in addition to my education, but she worked upon me as she could, dampening my citified nonchalance with a hearty dose of prairie conservatism. At the same time, quite unbeknownst to me, she was pulling strings across the pond to assure me a place among America's Kin.

The exact nature of any discussions in England are unknown to me, but later events convinced me that at least Lady Ellen Terry, vampiric Mistress of the City in the guise of an "ageless" theater star, and the entrepreneur Cecil Rhodes had taken part. ("Entrepreneur" seems a limited description for the nation builder, financier, and in my opinion at least, thoroughly unpleasant man that he was). Therefore, though I cannot vouch for specific wordplay, I'm confident that my re-creation of the tenor of those conversations is not far off the mark.

Rhodes was seeking assistance. His efforts to expand his influence in Africa were being opposed by King Lobengula of the Matabele, and he was exploring the possible impacts of Kindred aid. Lady Terry had imposed upon him in the past as needed, and with full knowledge of each other, they formed a frightful power base in London's—and England's—politics.

"Certainly you know what I seek," Rhodes must have begun, in a peculiar wheezy, high-pitched voice so striking in such a large man. "Though old Loben has effectively signed over much of Matabele land to me, he has little understanding of the niceties of such negotiations and I believe will resist any efforts to close the deal, as it were."

Lady Terry would have been unflappable, and would have at first sought to calm her excitable companion. "There is no question that we can offer aid," she would have assured him, "I'm of a mind to export talent for this endeavor. One of my American associates believes she has just the candidate, and can direct her to our shores posthaste."

Rhodes was a consummate nationalist, and had developed suspicion to a fine art. "Surely," he said, "you have some homegrown monster that would be up to the challenge?"

She waved the hidden accusation off languidly.

"Of course," she said, "but hear me out. Should the venture succeed, the nationality of our cat's paw will be quickly forgotten in the huzzahs directed at you. If she fails, well, it will be seen as just another example of the thoughtless intrusion of our American cousins, if it is not forgotten entirely in the noise of the wars that will undoubtedly follow."

"Oh, war there will most certainly be," answered the financier. "What I seek from you is assurance that we will win it when it arrives."

"Let's see what Clover's champion has to offer," the Lady replied. "I'll arrange for you to meet with her—perhaps drawing the Holmes boys into the discussion—and we can make our final decision at that time. Needless to say, I would not be averse to increasing my standing among those on the other side of the great ocean."

All this was, of course, hidden to me at the time. So when Mamie Clover completed my training and suggested that it might be best for me to absent myself from American shores for a time ("Out of sight, out of mind," I believe she said), I accepted the tickets readily and set off on what I was sure would be the beginning of a great adventure.

BRUCE WOODS

Bruce Woods is a professional writer/editor with more than 30 years in magazine publishing, having worked as editor of *Mother Earth News* and *Alaska Magazine*, among others, and has published both nonfiction and poetry books. *Prairie Schooner* magazine featured his work in its "Writing from Alaska" issue. His *Birdhouse Book*, brought out by Sterling/Lark, is still in print and has sold more than 100,000 copies.

After leaving the editor's position at *Alaska Magazine* in late 1998, Woods began a second career in External Affairs for the Alaska Region of the U.S. Fish and Wildlife Service. Eventually serving as the de facto writer/editor for the agency's largest region, as well as providing information and an initial contact point for state, national, and international media on topics affecting Alaska's often controversial wildlife and land management issues, Woods retired in the spring of 2013 in order to focus on fiction writing.

His *Hearts of Darkness* trilogy is scheduled for publication by Penmore Press.

In addition to the *Birdhouse Book* referenced above, Woods has published three nonfiction volumes and several books of poetry with small presses. During his magazine editing career he also served as editor/contributor to numerous nonfiction volumes. Several of his essays have been anthologized, as well.

Woods currently lives in Anchorage, Alaska with his wife Mary and his two cats, Lucy Fur and Boswell. Gardening and bicycling (the latter usually upon a single-speed road bike named "Yellow Snow" that he built from an old track frame bought online) are chief among his many interests outside of reading and writing. He has two children, Ethan, who studied music composition at Bennington College and now resides in Asheville, N.C., and his daughter Alice, who recently graduated from Minneapolis College of Art and Design and currently lives in Minneapolis.

ROYAL BLOOD

by

Bruce Woods

Historical and fictional characters come together and change the future of Africa forever. Renowned actress Lady Ellen Terry, detective Sherlock Holmes, financier Cecil Rhodes, hunter/naturalist Frederick Courtney Selous, King Lobengula, and a mysterious, undead adventuress named Paulette Monot become chess pieces in the Great Game, which takes the form of Africa's First Matabele War.

"It is unlikely that anyone will ever read this. In fact, if you are perusing these pages, and you're not one of the Kin ("vampires" to the uninitiated), it is almost certain that there's either been some sort of terrible mistake or that I (Miss Paulette Monot) have decided to take a mortal lover. The latter is perhaps more likely. Lucky you."

penmorepress.com

The Chosen Man

by

J. G Harlond

From the bulb of a rare flower bloom ambition and scandal

Rome, 1635: As Flanders braces for another long year of war, a Spanish count presents the Vatican with a means of disrupting the Dutch rebels' booming economy. His plan is brilliant. They just need the right man to implement it.

They choose Ludovico da Portovenere, a charismatic spice and silk merchant. Intrigued by the Vatican's proposal—and hungry for profit—Ludo sets off for Amsterdam to sow greed and venture capitalism for a disastrous harvest, hampered by a timid English priest sent from Rome, accompanied by a quick-witted young admirer he will use as a spy, and bothered by the memory of the beautiful young lady he refused to take with him.

Set in a world of international politics and domestic intrigue, *The Chosen Man* spins an engrossing tale about the Dutch financial scandal known as tulip mania—and how decisions made in high places can have terrible repercussions on innocent lives.

PENMORE PRESS
www.penmorepress.com

A Gathering of Vultures

Donald Michael Platt

Murder, mutilation, and carrion.... in paradise?

"There shall the vultures also be gathered, every one with her mate." - ISAIAH 34:15

Professional ballroom dancers Terri and Rick Hamilton aspire to be world champions. Unfortunately, Terri's recurring back and health problems place that goal well out of reach. They travel to Terri's birthplace, Florianópolis, on the scenic island of Santa Catarina off the coast of Brazil to vacation and visit their best friends and mentors.

Along the picturesque beaches, dead penguins and eviscerated bodies wash up on the shores of paradise, and Antarctic blasts play counterpoint to the tropical storms that rock the island. The scenic wonder is home not only to urubús, a unique sub-species of the black vulture, but also to a clique of mysterious women who offer Terri perfect health and the promise of fame—at a terrible price.

PENMORE PRESS
www.penmorepress.com

ASSASSINS OF ALAMUT
BY
JAMES BOSCHERT

An Epic Novel of Persia and Palestine in the Time of the Crusades

The Assassins of Alamut is a riveting tale, painted on the vast canvas of life in Palestine and Persia during the 12th century.

On one hand, it's a tale of the crusades—as told from the Islamic side—where Shi'a and Sunni are as intent on killing Ismaili Muslims as crusaders. In self-defense, the Ismailis develop an elite band of highly trained killers called Hashshashin whose missions are launched from their mountain fortress of Alamut.

But it's also the story of a French boy, Talon, captured and forced into the alien world of the assassins. Forbidden love for a princess is intertwined with sinister plots and self-sacrifice, as the hero and his two companions discover treachery and then attempt to evade the ruthless assassins of Alamut who are sent to hunt them down.

It's a sweeping saga that takes you over vast snow-covered mountains, through the frozen wastes of the winter plateau, and into the fabulous cites of Hamadan, Isfahan, and the Kingdom of Jerusalem.

"A brilliant first novel, worthy of Bernard Cornwell at his best."—Tom Grundner

PENMORE PRESS
www.penmorepress.com

DRAGON BLOOD
BY
BRUCE WOODS

Paulette is sent on a mission to China with the words of her mentor ringing in her ears. "A hot wind is now fanning the flames of racism in China, Paulette." Said Lady Ellen Terry. "And, like dust in a drought, it has blown up an army. They call themselves 'the boxers' society of righteous and harmonious fists,' or some variation thereof, and practice rituals that they claim bestow invulnerability and more. They are ill-armed and poorly trained but potentially numberless.

"Recently an auxiliary movement has sprung up. Reportedly consisting of young virgin women, from the ages of 12 to 18 and accounted uncommonly beautiful. They carry the name "Red Lanterns," and claim the powers of flight, fire-starting, and miraculous healing. It is these I wish you to investigate for any sign of Kindred activity.

PENMORE PRESS
www.penmorepress.com